Dancing
Queen

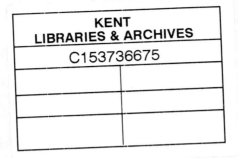

KINGFISHER

First published 2009 by Kingfisher
an imprint of Macmillan Children's Books
a division of Macmillan Publishers Limited
20 New Wharf Road, London N1 9RR
Basingstoke and Oxford
Associated companies throughout the world
www.panmacmillan.com

ISBN 978-0-7534-1765-2

Text copyright © Cathy Hopkins 2009
Cover illustration copyright © Monica Laita 2009
The right of Cathy Hopkins to be identified as the
author of this work has been asserted by her in accordance
with the Copyright, Designs and Patents Act 1988.

1 3 5 7 9 8 6 4 2
1TR/0209/MCK/SCHOY/60HLM/C

A CIP catalogue record for this book is available from the British Library.

Printed and Bound in the UK by CPI Mackays, Chatham ME5 8TD

Dancing Queen

Cathy Hopkins

KINGFISHER

Chapter One

Hairtastic

'You're not really going to do it, are you?' asked Lois, after Mum had finally left for the supermarket and Lois and I were alone in the house. I nodded as we watched Mum through the window in the hall. She struggled with her umbrella against the October rain, closed the gate, got into the car and drove off.

I punched the air. 'Let's move,' I said. 'We've only three hours before the auditions.'

Lois gave me a salute then we raced along to the bathroom where I locked the door just in case Mum came back for any reason.

I handed Lois the rubber gloves and the bleach that I'd been hiding in a carrier bag in my rucksack for the last few days. 'Here. Hold these while I wet my hair. And don't worry. I phoned Mum's hairdresser and she gave me very clear instructions. All I have to do is bleach my colour out, which might take a couple of applications, then put on a toner and bingo: white hair.'

'But, Marsha, your lovely red hair,' she objected. 'What if it goes green or something?'

I laughed. 'I'll deal with it. Everyone's always saying that we ought to go green these days.'

'That's not what I meant, dingbat brain. And where's your dad? What if he turns up?'

'Chill, Lois. He plays rugby every Saturday morning, and both my sisters are out with mates. It will be fine. Trust me. I'm not going green – I'm going white.'

Through the mirror to my left, I saw Lois glance at me anxiously. We made a curious pair. Lois with her long straight blonde hair and me with my shoulder-length red curls that try as I might always looked unruly. I looked like an urchin with a cheeky face standing next to a princess with dreamy eyes. 'Red hair is not right for the part and I have to get that part.'

Lois sighed and sat on the edge of the bath. She knew better than to argue with me when I wanted something and I wanted the part of the Ice Queen in the school show badly.

'Why is it so important to bleach your hair?' she asked.

'Don't you know anything?' I asked. 'If an actor is serious about a role, they have to live and breathe the part, tap into their secret self, dredge up old experiences to make it real. It's called method acting.'

'When did you experience being an Ice Queen?'

'Hmm. I suppose I haven't, but . . . I can imagine what it would be like to be an Ice Queen; I guess that's the next best thing.'

'And bleaching your hair white is method acting?'

'Methodish. It's like some actors put on weight or take it off for a part. I'm trying to become my character so that it will be more than acting. She will be an extension of myself. Like a part of me.'

Lois rolled her eyes. 'But you won't have to act. All you have to do is dance.' She laughed and added, 'And lure Oliver Blake . . .'

'Swoon, swoon,' I said. One of us always said that when anyone mentioned Oliver's name. He's the school babe and is totally hunky.

'. . . into your arms,' Lois continued. 'That's really why you want the role, isn't it?'

'Only partly,' I said. I did have a crush on Oliver but then so did the whole school and I knew he would think a girl in Year Seven way too young for him. 'It's also a way of being in the play and having an excuse to hang around with the drama group and, yeah, you're right, Oliver, swoon . . .'

'Swoon,' we chorused.

'. . . without having to kill myself or learn loads of lines. You know how I get bored so easily.' (Or have no staying power, as my mum would say.)

'Unlike some of us,' said Lois, who was going up for

a speaking part and had spent the best part of last week memorizing huge chunks of the play. 'I don't get it. You've never been that bothered about being in a show before.'

'Yeah, but that was before I realized that I want to be in the entertainment business.'

Lois rolled her eyes to the ceiling again. 'I thought you wanted to be an Olympic gymnast.'

'That was last week.'

'No. Last week you wanted to be a champion tennis player.'

'No. That was the week before. A girl can change her mind, can't she? In fact, ours is the age for dipping in and trying different things – our teachers say that all the time. And this week I am utterly convinced that I want to be on the stage.'

There was another reason that I wanted the part, though. Word had been going around school that Oliver's parents would be attending: Mr and Mrs Blake. But I was most interested in Mr Blake. Everyone at our school knew who he was. Michael Blake, agent to the stars. He was Mr Show Business and could make or break a person's career. Hearing that he was going to be there is what swung wanting to be in the show for me. It could be the stepping stone to a whole new life. A life of glamour and fame. Oliver was already a celebrity. He had been an extra in three

Christmas blockbusters and he even had a line to say in the last one. As soon as I heard that, I knew I had to go for it. I was born to be famous. Everyone says so, not just me.

I followed Katie's instructions to the letter and the last part was to apply the toner then wait.

'Fifteen minutes,' I said. 'A quick blow dry then we can go.'

'OK, then let's look at our horoscopes while we wait,' Lois suggested. 'Maybe it will tell us if we're going to get parts in the play. I found a really good website last night. Open your computer and I'll show you.'

Lois was always trying out New Age-type things like astrology and fortune telling. She says it's because she's an Aquarian and they are into stuff like that. I'm not convinced by it, but it can be fun to read my horoscope, especially if it says something good.

'Good idea,' I said. 'Let's see vot ze stars haf to say.'

We went into my room where I switched on my laptop and made way for Lois to sit at my desk by the window. I stretched and yawned before flopping on to my bed and kicking one of the turquoise cushions to the floor. 'God, I wish we could move sometimes. This house is so small!'

'No, it's not,' said Lois. 'Your mum and dad have made it really cosy here and I love your room since you painted it pale blue.' I knew she was only being polite.

She lived in an enormous Georgian house with high ceilings and large square rooms – her family even had two bathrooms, one with a bath and one with a shower, and they had a kitchen area at the back that opened into a conservatory. I loved going there; it felt so light and spacious. With five of us living here, our house felt like we were all squashed in. We only had one bathroom which drove me mad when there was a queue (which there usually was in the morning). I wished Mum and Dad would move, but they seem happy with pokey rooms and what they call a galley kitchen at the back downstairs. Personally I am made for bigger, better things and one day the world will realize this.

Lois typed in the web address.

'Who first?' she asked.

'Me me me,' I said. 'I can't wait to find out what it says.'

A page showing a starry night sky came into view and then a form asking for time of birth, date of birth and place.

'Born here,' I said. 'Second of April, seven fifteen in the morning. I remember because Mum always moans that I kept her awake all night.'

Lois typed in my name and my details and seconds later the laptop began to shake like a mobile on vibrate setting. The screen began to glow and then looked as if it had burst into flames with red, orange and yellow flickers of fire dancing in front of our eyes.

'Wow!' I exclaimed.

'Ohmigod, sorry,' said Lois, who didn't look impressed. She looked worried. 'I . . . I must have pressed something wrong.'

Suddenly, out of the fire, a golden banner appeared with a message saying, 'Congratulations, Marsha! You are this month's Zodiac Girl!'

'Oh!' said Lois. 'What's this all about?'

'Meeee. Yahey. I'm a Zodiac Girl.' I leaped up and did a karate-type kick into the air. 'Hazah.'

Lois laughed, and I looked back at the screen where a second banner appeared saying, 'As an Aries, your sign is ruled by the planet Mars.' Music began to play, drums then trumpets rising in volume and getting so loud that Lois put her hands over her ears.

'Turn it down,' she said, and I leaned over her and attempted to turn the volume down, but it didn't appear to work – the loud music continued.

'Oh, pooey, never mind all the fancy schmancy stuff,' I said. 'What have I got in store for me this month?'

A third banner appeared saying, 'As a typical Aries, you are always in a hurry to move on to the next best thing . . .'

Lois laughed. 'That's true,' she said as I continued reading the screen.

'Slow down or else Uranus, who features strongly in your chart at the beginning of this month, will steer you in an unexpected direction.' I glanced down the screen. 'Nothing about winning a major role in a play? Or . . . hold on, here's another bit.'

'As this month's Zodiac Girl,' it continued on the screen, 'this could be the most special four weeks of your whole life. A turning point. Your guardian will contact you. Make of it what you will.'

'Guardian? What guardian? What's that about?' I asked.

Lois shrugged. 'Don't know.'

'Oo, spooky,' I said, and put on my Russian spy accent. 'Make of eet vot you vill. This is a strange site, Lois.'

'I know. It's weird. It certainly didn't do that when I looked before. Maybe it's a promotion or something to bring in more users. Website designers are always looking for new tricks.'

'Yeah, but hey. The most special four weeks of my life? A turning point? That has to mean the play, doesn't it? I think it's a really good forecast.'

'But what about the Zodiac Girl thing?' asked Lois.

I shrugged. 'Dunno. You're the astrology expert.'

'Not really. I bet it's something like you were the thousandth person to punch in your details. If we'd done me first, it would be telling me that I'm a Zodiac Girl.'

'That's what I reckon,' I said. 'Do yours, do yours.'

Lois punched in her details. Moments later, the page showed a horoscope but there were no banners or music. 'This month looks to be a busy time and creative urges are strong now. Keep yourself focused and make time to recharge. Duh. How boring is that?'

'Anything else?' I asked. Then, 'A time for change: go shopping or get a new pet,' I read off the screen.

Lois shrugged. 'I was thinking of getting another goldfish, so I guess it's accurate enough. But you are so lucky, Marsha. All the good things happen to you.'

I smiled. 'I know. I am lucky. And I feel in my bones that this is going to be an amazing time.' I stood up as straight as I could and lifted my right arm up and pointed out of the window and up at the sky. 'I AM ZODIAC GIRL. Hiii YAH!' I did another karate-type kick. 'Mess with me and you mess with the PLANETS!' I chopped at the air around me. 'Hoi. Hoi. HOI.'

Lois glanced at her watch. 'Oops. It's time, Marsha.'

'Ohmigod. I hope my hair's turned out OK.' We raced to the bathroom and I began to rinse off the toner. Halfway through the process there was a loud knocking on the door.

'Oh no!' said Lois. 'We've been rumbled.'

'Who is it?' I asked in my best casual voice.

'The big bad bogie,' my sister Cissie called back.

'Hurry up, you idiot. I need the loo and so does Eleanor. Get a move on. Sandy's dad is waiting in the car for us outside.'

'Can't, I'm busy,' I said.

'You've got two seconds, Marsha,' Eleanor called, 'or your life won't be worth living. What are you doing in there anyway?'

'Nothing,' said Lois.

'So let us in,' said Eleanor.

'I'd better open the door,' I said, 'or else they might make trouble.' I quickly pulled a towel over my head and unlocked the bathroom door. Cissie and Eleanor were standing there looking annoyed and suspicious. They always look at me like that – it's part of the price I pay for being the youngest sister.

'Yes. What were you doing in here, kid?' asked Cissie as Eleanor shoved past her.

'Um. Hair wash and then we're doing makeovers and don't call me kid,' I said.

'OK, kid,' said Cissie. I wanted to punch her but resisted because I wanted her to go.

'You have fab hair,' said Lois, putting her hand up to touch Cissie's long red locks, which she was wearing loose down her back. 'You three are so lucky. I wish my hair was such a gorgeous colour.' Good tactic, I thought as Lois gushed on about the Leibowitz red hair. All three of us girls have inherited it from Mum and

Cissie was a sucker for flattery.

Eleanor wasn't long in the bathroom and flew straight down the stairs without even giving us a second glance then Cissie went in. Loud beeping from their mate Sandy's dad's car horn on the road outside prevented Cissie from hanging about too long either, so minutes later we were back in the bathroom.

'Phew,' I said. 'That was close.'

'I know,' said Lois. She looked worried. 'You've had the toner on about ten minutes longer than you should have.'

'It will be OK,' I said, and leant over the bath so I could rinse my hair. Once done, I towelled my hair and then looked in the mirror.

'Wow!' said Lois.

'Superyummingdoopah!' I gasped. My hair looked amazing. Katie's advice had worked a treat and my hair was as white as snow. The texture felt a little brittle, probably because of the two applications of bleach, but overall it was a great result.

'It makes your eyes look so blue, even bluer than before,' said Lois. 'And it makes your skin look really pale. Perfect for the Ice Queen.'

I nodded then ran some gel through so my hair slicked right back off my face. As I did so, a few strands of hair came out. 'Oops,' I said as I put them in the bin. So I'd lost a few hair strands. The effect was perfect. It not only looked cool but also made me look like I was from another planet.

Mum was going to kill me.

Chapter Two

Star Pupil

'I'm at the back,' I said to Lois, after we'd registered with the drama teacher, Mr Sanderson, at the gym where the auditions were being held. He had taken our names and directed us to different areas that were already filling up with eager wannabes. Dancers at the back of the hall, speaking parts up on the stage, scenery people and technicians to the left, costumes to the right.

'Laters,' said Lois, and she took off in the direction of the stage.

Mrs Pierson, our PE teacher, was waiting for us at the back and smiled when she saw me – I am one of her favourite pupils and PE is one of my best subjects. I sometimes wonder if PE is her best subject, though, because she doesn't look as though she does much of it. She is a small stocky lady with an enormous chest and thick legs, and, if she moves too quickly, she gets out of breath. With her were six girls from Years Eight and Nine at our school. I gave them a wave and a couple of them smiled and waved back. Most of them looked nervous even though we'd had a run-through of the routine last week one night after school.

'Whatever happened to your hair, dear?' Mrs Pierson asked.

'I did it for the part. It will wash out easy peasy,' I lied.

'That's the attitude. I like to see that my girls have tried to get into role.'

One of the girls from Year Eight smiled weakly at me. She looked like she was going to be sick.

'I wish I'd thought of that,' said another of the girls.

'Now, let's get started,' said Mrs Pierson when it became clear that there weren't going to be any more contenders. She turned to the CD player on the table behind her. 'We'll go alphabetically so that means Grace Anderson – you're up first.'

A small girl with long dark hair tied back in a plait got up and when Mrs Pierson switched on the CD player a piece of classical music began to play and Grace began to go through the routine. She fluffed a few steps and then lost her timing so Mrs Pierson switched the music off and let her begin again, but it was clear that she wasn't going to get the part. She was way too clodhoppy. I quickly assessed who else was up for it and saw that all their names came before mine in the alphabet, which meant that I would be last to audition. Excellent, I thought, that means I can watch what the others do and it also gives me a chance to see the routine over and over so by the time it is my turn I should know it really well. To my side, I could see Carol Kennedy watching Grace and counting the steps under her breath. Carol would be my main competitor. She did ballet out of school, and everyone knew that she was a good dancer. I used to do ballet in junior school but got bored with it after a few years and let it go when I got to secondary school, and got into playing more competitive sport instead. However, when I began to learn the routine for the show, I was surprised at how easily the steps came back.

After Grace was Mary. I had to stop myself giggling as she had no sense of timing or rhythm. This is like watching auditions for the X Factor, I thought, as Mary almost tripped over her own feet.

After Mary was Phoebe, who was OK but not really Ice Queen material. There was something about her that was too timid. After her was Ellie the goth, then Tara. Tara was pretty good, the best so far.

'Carol. You're next,' said Mrs Pierson, and Carol got to her feet, took up first position and went into the routine. I had to admit that she danced gracefully, light as a feather. How can I make my audition stand out? I asked myself as I watched her pirouette around the gym. What would mark me as the Ice Queen above the others? I thought about what I knew about the play so far. It had been written by a boy in the Sixth Form called James O'Malley, and the dance sequence was to be in the second act when the main character, played by Ollie (swoon, swoon), gets stranded in a forest in winter in the snow. As he battles on, his life slips away and he falls into a trance and dreams of an Ice Queen and her princesses who try to lure him to his death. A bit like how mermaids used to try and lure sailors to their death in some legends. It's a totally dramatic story and I couldn't help but think that Carol's performance, although good, was too lightweight. She looked like a fairy princess who wouldn't harm a fly.

Carol finished and the other girls clapped. She flushed a little and smiled at them. It ain't over yet, I thought as Mrs Pierson called me to go next.

I took up first position as Carol had done and breathed deeply into my abdomen the way that I'd been taught when I used to do ballet. Stand tall, I told myself. Remember that you're a queen. And not just any queen, you are the Ice Queen with a heart that is cold and cruel.

I went into the routine and, as I did, I narrowed my eyes and I glared at Mrs Pierson and the other girls as if they were beneath me and I was thinking about killing them. My heart is full of icicles, I thought, as I danced and tried to convey that I was dangerous as well as queenly.

'And a one, two, three, excellent, lovely,' cooed Mrs Pierson as the music came to an end. As they had for Carol, the girls clapped for me. I noticed that Carol didn't clap, though. She gave me a fake smile when I glanced over at her.

'That was so cool,' said Phoebe. 'You looked scary. Like, in control but there was an air of don't mess with me.'

'Good,' I said, 'because that's what I was going for.'

Mrs Pierson clapped her hands. 'Now, class,' she said, 'I want you all to watch Marsha Leibowitz and then do the routine exactly the way she does it and then I will decide who gets the part.' She gave me a nod and a smile. 'Go ahead, Marsha dear.'

I went through the routine again and, soon after, the others copied me and I could see Carol narrowing her eyes and glaring with all her might, but instead of looking evil she looked as if she had just sucked a lemon.

After we'd done the routine once more, Mrs Pierson clapped her hands again. 'OK, girls. I have made my decision. Marsha Leibowitz, you shall be our Ice Queen and Carol, Tara and Phoebe the princesses. Mary, Ellie and Grace, I am sure we can find you something to do. So rehearsals start next Wednesday after school.' She glanced in my direction and gave me a wink.

There were a few sighs of disappointment, but Tara and Phoebe came over and congratulated me. 'Thanks,' I said. 'And I'm so glad you got parts too.'

I looked over at Carol who was staring at the floor. She didn't look up or make any comments. I shrugged and turned to leave when Mrs Pierson clapped her hands again. 'Attention, girls in the show, hang on a second. There's someone I want you to meet.'

She motioned to someone at the front of the gym and when I turned to see who it was I saw a tall black man wave back and begin to make his way over.

'Hubba hubba,' Phoebe whispered in my ear as he got closer. He was very handsome with a square jaw and cheekbones to die for. As he crossed the gym, everyone turned to look at him. He radiated charisma like he was a Hollywood movie star.

Mrs Pierson flushed pink. 'Girls, this is Mario Ares,' she said in a curiously squeaky voice. 'He's going to be working here part time and taking some classes after school in fitness and self-defence. If any of you feel you'd like to sign up, I think that would be an excellent idea.'

Mr Ares stared at me as if he knew me from somewhere and was trying to remember. 'Ice Queen,' he said.

Mrs Pierson nodded. 'And the other girls will be her princesses. Marsha is our star PE pupil, aren't you, Marsha dear?'

I nodded. 'It's my favourite subject.'

Mr Ares smiled. 'It would be. Aries are good at sport.'

'Wow! How did you know that I was an Aries?'

Mr Ares smiled. 'I'm good at spotting star signs.'

'What am I?' said Phoebe.

'Pisces,' he replied, and looked at the other girls. 'And you two are . . . Libra and . . . Cancer.'

'And me?' asked Mrs Pierson.

'Capricorn,' said Mr Ares without a second of hesitation. He flashed her a smile. 'Hardworking.'

Mrs Pierson sighed. 'Tell me about it. Gosh, you really have a gift for this.'

'Ah, but did you know that I am not just an Aries,' I said. 'I am also . . .' I jumped around in a circle ending with a karate kick. 'Zodiac Girl.'

'As a matter of fact, I did,' said Mr Ares.

'Yeah, right,' I said. I knew he didn't. He couldn't. He was just being clever. 'So what does that mean, then?'

Mr Ares looked up over my right shoulder as if reading an invisible screen. 'It means . . . Mars, Saturn and Pluto are conjunct. It means you have a major life lesson to learn. Oh, and an encounter with Uranus, so that means it may come about in an unexpected way. The planet Uranus is unpredictable, to say the least.' He said it with such seriousness and then looked directly into my eyes as if he were looking right into the core of me. It sent a shiver down my spine.

'Oo. Major life lesson? Don't we all?' asked Mrs Pierson with a giggle. 'OK, girls, on your way. And we'll see you Wednesday.'

Three planets conjunct and an encounter with another. That does sound major. Superyummingdoopah, I thought as I pulled my eyes away from Mr Ares and headed for the door. Lois was still busy up on the stage, but I managed to catch her eye and gave her the thumbs up. She gave me the thumbs up back.

When I glanced over my shoulder, Mr Ares was still watching me. I gave him a wave. He wasn't going to intimidate me with his intense looks and mysterious sayings.

Chapter Three

Unexpected!

As I walked out of the gym, in my mind's eye, I could see exactly how it was going to unfold. It was going to be SPECTACULAR! Opening night, an audience buzzing with anticipation, boys in Year Eleven taking photos of the stars of the show for the school magazine, me me ME and Ollie being the centre of attention, all my family in the front rows, Mr Blake seeing my performance then asking, 'Who's that girl?' He'd get my number. I could feel myself getting more and more excited by the prospect of it all. Superyummingdoopah. Being chosen to be a Zodiac Girl was such a good omen and this was only the beginning of my star-studded month. Luckily the rain had stopped and the skies had brightened, reflecting my mood. I took a deep breath of the fresh air. As I continued on my way across the school playground and out towards the gates, I heard footsteps behind me.

'Hey, Marsha,' a voice called. I turned to see Sophie King running to catch up with me. She was in Year Ten at our school. A large girl with frizzy dark hair who hung out with the geeky set from her year.

'Hey,' she panted when she reached me. 'I . . . I . . . just got to catch my breath. Wuff, puff. I . . . I heard you got the part of the Ice Queen?'

'Yeah. Yeah, I did.'

'I saw you across the gym. You were brill.'

'Thanks, Sophie.'

'Thing is, I'm organizing a charity event to be held at the end of the month and I wondered if you could help.'

'Charity? What for?'

'My cousin works at the hospital out near Osbury and she's asked me to help her raise money for a recreation wing in the children's section.'

'Oh, OK. Of course.' I reached into my pocket. 'I . . . I'm really sorry, I haven't got much money on me,' I said as I drew out a twenty-pence piece. 'I could maybe give you some more next week after I've got my pocket money.'

'No,' said Sophie. 'I don't want your money. I want your talent.'

'Talent? What do you mean?'

'We need acts for the show to draw in the crowds and when I saw you I thought you'd be fantastic.'

'Oh! Who have you got so far?'

Sophie grimaced. 'Not many, to tell the truth. In fact, only my younger brother doing a magic act, which between you and me is rubbish, and a few deadbeats from Year Seven who want to read their poetry, which is so bad it makes me want to lie on the floor and tear my hair out. That's why I'm asking you. Someone with a bit of charisma to pull in the crowds.'

Although I felt flattered, I was reluctant to get involved. Most days were packed with activities: tennis on a Monday, badminton on Tuesday, there would be rehearsals for the show on Wednesday evening from now on, karate on Thursday, and Fridays I had to use to catch up on homework. My life was very full. 'Um . . . I . . . Um, listen, Sophie, can I think about it and get back to you?'

Sophie gave me a strange look and I realized that I must have sounded a bit precious. 'I . . . getting the part has only just happened and I don't know what's involved yet, you know, in the way of rehearsals as well as Wednesdays. Time wise I will have to put in extra to make it work. And, besides, life is pretty full on at the mo.'

Sophie's expression registered weariness. Even her shoulders had slumped as if she had the weight of the world on them. 'Whatever,' she said. 'It's really hard to get anyone to do anything like this.'

'I bet loads of people will want to get involved when you ask them?' (Just not me, I thought.) 'Um, let me think about it, yeah?'

Sophie turned away. 'Yeah, sure. Later, then.'

As we continued our separate ways, I think we both knew that I wasn't going to be taking part in her non-event. I did feel a twinge of guilt, though, and was grateful when I went to wait at the bus stop that Lois joined me soon after. She was as excited as I was because she had got the part she wanted in the play and after we'd both relived every moment of our auditions to each other I filled her in on Sophie's request.

'Are you going to do it?' she asked.

'Don't think so. I don't want to. My life is like, soooo busy. That's OK, isn't it? I mean, she'll find people. It's, like, celebrities get millions of requests every day and they have to pick and choose which they do and don't do.'

Lois creased up laughing. 'Celebrities! Get you. It's only the school play we're in, Marsha.'

'So? One day I am going to be very famous, you watch, so you may laugh, but you'll see. In the meantime I have to learn to protect my talent and not let people drain me.'

'Drain you? It's a charity show! Get real.'

'Ah, but you say yes to one, you say yes to them all. Anyway, I heard Savannah Macauley—'

'Who's she?'

'Duh? Don't you know anything? She's a Hollywood A-list star, as in mega. I heard her do an interview on the telly. She said that she got drained by all the constant demands on her time and she also said that she had made some bad choices in the beginning of her career by saying yes to everyone. I took note for when I hit the big time.'

Lois collapsed with laughter and slid down the wall next to the bus stop as if what I'd said was so funny that she could hardly stand up. 'Marsha Leibowitz, you really are something.'

'I know,' I said, but I gave her a big grin to show that I wasn't really full of myself. I couldn't say yes to everyone who asked me to be in their shows. I was going to be in demand and I had to be choosy whether Lois understood or not. 'I will send her a donation from my pocket money.'

'How very generous of you,' said Lois.

'Aye thought so,' I said in a posh voice that sounded like the queen and made Lois laugh even more. 'But isn't it fab? We're both going to be in the show and Mr Blake will be there . . .'

A few moments later the bus came and we spent the rest of the journey gossiping about who else had got parts and sharing our fantasies about the show and the after-show party and what we were going to wear. By the time I got off at my stop I was feeling on top of the world, so I went into the post office corner shop to buy a curly chocolate chew to celebrate.

Mr Singh, who ran the shop, glanced up when I walked in. 'Hi, Marsha,' he said.

'Hey, Mr Singh,' I replied.

'I'm glad you came by,' he said, and slipped off his stool to reach into a huge postbag behind the counter. 'I got a package for you.'

'For me?'

He handed me a parcel wrapped in deep red paper with a white label. 'Marsha Leibowitz, Zodiac Girl,' it said clearly in bright red letters.

'Oh, what is it?' I asked.

'Why don't you open it and find out?' Mr Singh replied, and then turned to serve a customer who had come in behind me.

I ripped off the paper to find two small boxes inside tied with red ribbon. I opened the smaller first. Inside was a silver chain with a tiny charm hanging on it. On closer inspection I saw that it was a ram's head, which I knew was the symbol for the star sign of Aries. Cute, I thought, and put it on immediately. Whatever was in the second parcel was wrapped in bubble wrap so took a bit longer to unwrap.

'Wow! It's a mobile phone,' I said when I'd ripped off the last bit of paper. I held it up to the light. It was exquisite, with amazing colours – deep blood red and orange – like fire. At the top of the phone, above the screen, was a dark stone that looked black at first, but, if you looked closely, appeared to have layers of deeper colour shining through.

'Bloodstone,' said Mr Singh. 'Very beautiful. Who's it from?'

'No idea,' I replied. 'I think I may have won it on an astrology website.'

'Lucky you,' said Mr Singh. 'Shall I put the wrappings in the bin?'

I shook my head. 'No, I'll take it in case there's an address for the sender so I can thank them,' I said. I pocketed the phone and headed out for the pavement.

This really is my lucky day, I thought as I felt the smooth surface of the new phone in my pocket next to my old one. A part in the play, a present in the post and a curly chocolate chew. Life really doesn't get any better.

I couldn't resist. There was a knee-high wall to my right. I stepped up and, putting one foot in front of the other, I pretended that I was on a tightrope. I put my arms out to my sides the way I had seen performers do in the circus.

'You look happy,' called a man on a cycle on the other side of the road. He seemed to have appeared from nowhere. I looked over and did a double take at his strange appearance. He had spiked-up white hair, a silver lightning fork painted on his forehead, shiny electric-blue clothes and his bike wasn't a two wheeler – it was a unicycle. He looked as if he were going to a sci-fi fancy-dress party.

'I am happy.' I grinned back at him and the moment our

eyes met a dog barked a short distance away. Seconds later, there was the sound of a cat screeching, frantic scrabbling and then a ginger tom, spitting and hissing, shot out in front of me. It sprang off the wall, down the pavement and round a corner. It all happened so fast.

'Ee . . . yoh, wuh, arrgh . . .' I cried as I lost my balance. I put my left hand out to stop my fall and landed in a crumpled heap by the wall.

The man was off his bike and by my side like a shot. 'Oops! Oh. Are you all right? Can you get up? Stupid cat. Did you see it?'

'I . . . I . . .' Something was wrong. I put my hand out to try and push myself up on to my knees, but I yowled in pain as my left wrist crumpled like the bone had turned to rubber. 'I-I'm OK, but . . . I think I hurt my wrist.'

'Then don't move,' said the man. 'Is there someone I can phone?'

I nodded and with my right hand I pulled out my usual mobile. 'It's OK. I-I'll phone my mum, but please don't go.'

The man looked at me with kind eyes. 'I won't leave,' he said.

And then the tears came. My wrist hurt badly.

The man knelt down next to me. 'Came out of nowhere it did,' he said as he patted my shoulder. 'Most unexpected!'

Chapter Four

Spook Night

'Now this is how you do tightrope,' said the man, who had introduced himself as Uri after I'd made my call to Mum.

'No,' I cried as he lifted his unicycle on to the wall, then got up and sat on the seat. 'You'll fall too.'

He winked. 'Me? Never. Just watch,' he said, and he began to ride along the narrow edge of the wall. After a few moments, he sprang up and stood on the seat. I wanted to clap, but didn't dare in case it hurt my wrist even more. It was throbbing like mad and I was worried that I might have broken it.

'Whoa,' I called as Uri bent over and did a handstand. 'Whoa! Be careful!' He was awesome to watch. A bit mad, I thought, not someone you'd expect to run into on the way home, but impressive nonetheless. I wonder who he is. 'Are you going to a fancy-dress party?'

He laughed and shook his head.

'Children's entertainer?'

He shook his head again.

'Who then?'

'I am Uri, otherwise known as Uranus, ruler of Aquarius, planet of the unexpected.'

I laughed and did a wibbly-wobbly salute with my good hand and crossed my eyes. 'Yeah, right. And I'm Queen Zugula from the planet Zog. You're winding me up.'

He shrugged. 'Maybe. Maybe not.' He continued to ride back and forth along the wall while we waited for Mum and I was grateful for the distraction because I found myself forgetting that I was in pain as I watched him. It wasn't long before I saw Mum's grey car coming up the street behind him, her anxious face looking out of the window on the driver's side. As soon as she spotted me, she parked the car and leaped out. She'd obviously come straight from her Pilates class without changing because she was still in her black Lycra gym clothes and her red hair was tied up in a bun at the back of her head.

'Ohmigod!' she cried when she saw me sitting on the pavement. 'What have you done?' She turned to Uri who got down from the wall with his cycle. 'And who are you?'

'He's Uri and I've hurt my—' I started, but Mum was looking at Uri's hair and then she looked back at mine. In all the commotion, I'd forgotten that my hair was as white as his. 'Your hair, Marsha! WHAT have you done to your hair?' She turned back to Uri.

'What have you done to my daughter?'

'Nothing! He was just passing by when I fell. He kept me company. Never mind my hair. Never mind him, Mum. I'm in pain,' I groaned.

Uri nodded. 'I think she needs to go to the hospital,' he said, and pointed at the wall. 'I think she hurt her wrist.'

'Oh Lord, ohmigod!' Mum knelt down and asked me to wriggle my fingers and when she found that I couldn't she tried to help me up, but as I put weight on my right foot it crumpled beneath me.

'Ow, ow, my ankle,' I yelped. I realized that I must have fallen on it and twisted it.

'Lean on me,' said Mum.

'And take my arm with your good one,' said Uri. It was no use. I couldn't stand up properly, and Mum looked like she was going to faint.

'I'll lift her,' said Uri, and in a second his strong hands picked me up as if I were as light as a feather.

'Open the car door,' he said.

Mum opened the door and Uri positioned me gently in the front seat.

'Let me know how she is, won't you?' asked Uri, and as Mum got into the driver's seat he looked at me and said, 'Sorry, Zodiac Girl. I know it said in your chart that you had an encounter coming up with me.'

'What do you mean?'

'I told you,' said Uri. 'I'm Uranus, the planet of the

unexpected and . . . well, sometimes I don't even know what's going to happen.'

'I . . . who?' I started.

'What's he talking about?' Mum interrupted as she got into the driver's seat. 'Is he mad?' She closed the door then wound down the window. 'Be off with you. Shoo, you strange man.'

Uri raised an eyebrow in surprise and shrugged his shoulders at me.

'No, Mum, you don't understand. He's been kind,' I protested.

'So what's he on about, then? Uranus? Zodiacs?' Mum asked, starting the car.

'I don't know,' I replied, turning in my seat to watch Uri out of the window as we drove away. How did he know I was a Zodiac Girl? I wound down my window with my good hand. 'How did you know I was a Zodiac Girl,' I called back at him.

But it was too late. Uri was mouthing something, but I couldn't hear above the roar of the engine, and seconds later the car turned a corner and my mystery companion had disappeared.

Chapter Five

Casualty

'OWWWWWWWWW,' I yelped when the young doctor who had introduced himself as Dr Sam Heaton pressed on a few points around my wrist.

'OWWWWWWW,' he yelped back as my foot shot out in response to his prodding and kicked him on the shin.

'Oops, sorry,' I said.

'Th-th-that's OK,' Dr Sam stuttered, but his eyes watered and he manoeuvred himself out of the way of my feet. He hardly looked old enough to be a doctor; in fact, he looked more like he belonged in the Sixth Form with his pleasant face, tousled brown hair and pink cheeks.

'It hurt when you pressed,' I said.

'Is it broken?' asked Mum.

'I can't tell until it's been X-rayed. You hang on here and I'll go and get that organized. In the meantime, I'll get one of the nurses to give you a painkiller,' said Dr Sam, then I heard him mutter under his breath, 'Might even take one myself.'

'How long will it take?' I asked. 'I want to go home.'

We'd been in the accident and emergency unit for over three hours waiting to be seen. My wrist and my ankle were throbbing, I was hungry and I had a headache coming on.

'Not long,' he said, 'but it's always busy here at weekends.'

As he made his way out of the small cubicle, a teenage boy with red hair who was coming the other way suddenly lurched and then vomited all over Dr Sam's white coat.

'Eww! Gross!' I cried, and then clapped my hand over my mouth because I realized I'd said it so loud that everyone in the unit must have heard. Behind the counter, a man who was taking the names of newcomers chuckled. I reckoned I'd voiced what a lot of the people who work there daily must think. 'Remind me never to be a doctor,' I said to Mum.

'But thank God some people choose to be,' she replied, looking coyly in Dr Sam's direction, which almost made me say 'Gross!' again. I mean, eww, my mum acting like a teenage girl.

I watched Dr Sam retreat through the doors at the end of the corridor. 'I wonder if this is a typical day for him. Kicked and then someone throws up on you. What a job!'

After another hour of waiting and playing a word

game with Mum to pass the time, I was taken down to the X-ray unit. By then the tablet that a nurse had given me had taken effect, my wrist wasn't quite as painful and all I felt was that I'd like to slide under one of the chairs or beds and have a sleep. Once I'd been X-rayed, they saw that my ankle wasn't broken, so a nurse bandaged it up and I was shown to A&E again. We had to wait to see what was wrong with my wrist.

Being ill has to be the most boring thing ever, I thought, as Mum fussed over me before going off to get us some sandwiches and a drink from the shop near the hospital's main reception. I looked around for something to do, but couldn't see anything. I sat back in my chair and looked up at the ceiling. It was covered with white tiles and there was a crack in the one nearest the light bulb. I glanced back down and around. A few people were sitting on the orange plastic chairs in the waiting room, an old lady in her nightie, a fraught-looking mother with a chubby-cheeked toddler, a red-faced man who stank of beer and had a cut on his forehead. Opposite were the cubicles where the doctors saw the patients. Most of them had the curtains pulled closed. I looked across the unit and out of the window but couldn't see much from where I was. I was about to get my phone out when I saw a poster above a radiator that said the use of mobiles WAS NOT allowed. Seeing the sign reminded me of my new zodiac mobile. That's what I can do, I thought. I can see how it works. I felt in my pocket for the phone, but couldn't find it. I stood up and had another feel around. No, it definitely wasn't there. Had I put it somewhere? I wondered. No. No. I definitely had it in my pocket just before the cat jumped in front of me. Bug bottoms. It must have slipped out when I fell. Grrr. This day really is turning out to be a major bummer.

I got up and hobbled to the A&E reception desk and waited for what seemed like an eternity for the lady there to look at me.

Finally she glanced up and made eye contact. 'What?' she asked.

'Have you got any magazines or books or anything? I'm bored.'

'Does this look like a library? No, we haven't got any magazines. Where's your mother?'

'Gone to the shop.'

'Then maybe she'll get you a magazine.'

Her glare communicated that I was to go back to my seat, sit down and shut up. Hmm, I thought. She's a cross nick. I sat back, closed my eyes and tried not to focus on my wrist. It was beginning to hurt again. Try to have a nice daydream, I told myself. It's what Dad always advised me to do when I was little and we were on a long journey somewhere. Imagine that you're in a lovely place on holiday and the sea is just a metre away, lapping up on the shore. The sun is shining down, the birds are singing . . . My fantasy was disturbed by the sound of someone groaning and seconds later the powerful odour of disinfectant filled my nostrils. I opened my eyes to the bright lights above. At least I won't have to stay in overnight, I thought. I can't imagine that anyone ever gets any sleep.

As I sat there, an old man came into the unit. I couldn't help but stare at him because he seemed so out of place – I could see by his white hair and beard that he was old, but he seemed to radiate health as if he were lit up from the inside. He scanned the people in the waiting area and then the moment he saw me he nodded to himself and began to make his way over. He must be short sighted, I thought, because I have never set eyes on him in my life.

When he reached me, he pulled something out of his pocket and handed it over. 'I think this is yours,' he said.

It was my zodiac phone!

'Yes. I . . . H-how did you know?' I stuttered.

The man gave me a stern look. 'It is my duty to know. And you, young lady, ought to be more careful. To be chosen as a Zodiac Girl is a rare honour, as it is to receive one of these phones. To lose it on your very first day, well . . . it smacks of irresponsibility, if you ask me.'

'That's so unfair,' I blurted. 'I fell. It wasn't my fault. It must have slipped out of my pocket.'

'That's so unfair,' mimicked the man in a baby voice. 'Not my fault.'

'It wasn't. And I don't talk like that.'

'Major lesson in life, young lady, and that is take responsibility for your actions and your mistakes.'

I felt myself growing very cross. 'No need for the lecture,' I said with a pout.

He turned to go. 'Well, don't lose it again. I have better things to do with my time than chase silly young girls around with things they have lost. And do I hear a word of thanks? Not likely.'

'Thanks,' I said. I knew I sounded sulky, but I'd had a miserable day. He didn't understand. 'Hey. Who are you anyway?'

'Dr Cronus. Another one of the planets. You've met Mars and Uranus already. I've come by to let you know that as an Aries your ruling planet is Mars, so you get Mario Ares as your guardian. He's already made himself known to you, but you can expect him to be in touch again soon to help out where he can. A few of us others will also drop by from time to time to lend a helping hand.' He chuckled when he said this. 'Helping hand, that's exactly what you do need, isn't it?'

Oh, heckity thump, I thought, he's a nutty noodle job. Best humour him until Mum gets back and then we can call security. 'Oh, yes. Um . . . and which planet are you?'

He gave me another of his stern looks. 'Saturn. Saturn

rules Capricorn. It's a very different sign to Aries. Do you know much about your sign?'

I nodded. 'A bit. Good at sports. First sign of the zodiac, yeah?'

'Yes, not yeah. And impatient. Can't sit still. Should look before they leap. Not like Capricorns who think before they act,' he said, and pointed at my wrist. 'Still, this ought to slow down your momentum for a while.' I'm sure that it wasn't my imagination – he looked gleeful as he said it.

'It's nothing serious,' I said. 'I think it's just a sprain.'

Dr Cronus chuckled. 'I wouldn't bet on that!'

And then he stomped off.

What a strange man, I thought.

Mum came back a few moments later with two cartons of juice, a bar of chocolate and a packet of crisps.

'There wasn't much left in the shop,' she said as she put the items on an empty chair next to us.

I pointed to the glass doors. We could see Dr Cronus crossing the car park. 'See that man, Mum? He's a total nutter.'

Mum strained to look, shook her head and laughed. 'I don't think so, love. That's Dr Cronus.'

'You know him?'

Mum nodded. 'He's the headmaster of a very prestigious local school just outside Osbury. He has a fantastic reputation and gets great results. I met him at the last conference that was held for local headmasters and headmistresses. I was very impressed and think I'll use some of his methods in my school. He's very strict and old fashioned, but it works.'

'He thinks he's a planet.'

Mum laughed again and patted my arm. 'Honestly, Marsha, you do say some funny things sometimes.'

'No really. He thinks he's Saturn. Rules Capricorn. He just told me.'

It was no use. I tried telling her about Uri too, but she just creased up laughing as if I were making it all up on purpose to entertain her.

'Oh, for heaven's sake, Marsha,' she said. I had been about to show her my zodiac phone, but after her reaction I decided not to waste my time. I would investigate these planet people and the zodiac thing on my own.

'This really has to be the most boring day of my whole life,' I said, after we had sat for another age with nothing else to do but watch sick people come and go.

'Are you OK? Is there anything I can get you?' asked Mum.

'I just want to go home,' I said.

She put her hand over my good one and gave me a painful smile. 'Me too.'

We sat there for another hour while Mum put on her

cheerful face and voice, and tried to keep me entertained. I found myself nodding off while she rattled on, and woke with a jolt when I almost slipped off the chair. What's going on? I wondered as I heard Dr Sam's and Mum's voices a few feet away.

'Murmur murmur, murmur murmur.'

I strained to hear what they were saying. I could hear the odd word like ulna and fracture.

'I CAN hear you,' I said. 'I'm not deaf.'

Mum turned round. 'Sorry, darling. Dr Heaton here says it looks like a greenstick fracture.'

'Sounds like some kind of plant. Is it bad?' I asked.

Dr Sam gave me a smile. 'It's an incomplete fracture where the bone bends like a green stick. We'll have to put you in a backslab.'

'A backslab? What's that?'

'It's a plaster of Paris cast from the hand to halfway between the elbow and armpit. It's free on one side of the forearm to allow swelling and enable circulation.'

'How long before it gets better?' I asked as a feeling of alarm hit my stomach.

'Hmm. Fractures of the upper limb bones take about six weeks to heal—'

'Six weeks?'

'It can take around half of that in younger people. With a bit of luck you'll be up and whacking a tennis ball about again in four weeks.'

'Four weeks? Bu— but I'm in the school show. I'm the Ice Queen.'

Dr Sam and Mum exchanged worried glances.

'And when's the show?' asked the doctor.

'At the end of the month. In about three weeks.'

'Hmm. Depends on the part. I think we could strap you up and you'd be OK as long as you don't move around too much,' said Dr Sam.

'I don't say anything. I dance. I'm the main dancer. The Ice Queen.' I could feel my fantasy about being the star of the show and the talk of the school begin to crack and melt like an iceberg.

'Dance? Oh no,' said Dr Sam. 'I don't think there's going to be much chance of that. Your ankle won't take so long – it will be tender for a few weeks at least – but a greenstick fracture like yours needs time to recover properly.'

I can do this, I thought. I can fix this. I won't give up. I sat up and made myself snap out of the sluggish feeling that had come over me since I'd taken the painkiller. 'OK. So let's do it. Sooner we get out of here, the better and the sooner I can get on with my recovery.' I held out my wrist. 'Do your stuff, Doc.'

Dr Sam grimaced. 'I'm afraid you won't be going home today, Marsha. We need to keep you in tonight—'

'Stay in? Overnight? Noooo. You can't be serious. It's

not even a complete fracture – you just said so. Mum, tell him—'

'Darling, you have to do what the doctor says. What is it you have to do, Doctor?'

'She'll go up to the ward and be put into a Bradford sling. It holds the arm in the air. This is to reduce the swelling and makes the operation easier.'

'OPERATION! WARD? Whoa there a moment. What operation?'

'We need to manipulate the fracture. Don't worry, you'll be put to sleep so you won't feel it and it means we can do the manipulation without any need for surgical incision. We use traction and rotation, and then we'll put your arm in plaster of Paris from your knuckles to just above your elbow.'

A frightened voice was getting louder in the pit of my stomach. It just said one word: NoooooooooooOOOOOOOOOOOOOOOO!

'I . . . I . . . But . . .' The idea of anyone rotating, manipulating or coming anywhere near my sore wrist made me feel faint.

'How long will it take?' asked Mum.

'The operation will take about half an hour. And it won't be too painful afterwards.'

'Not too painful? I . . . No. No. I don't do pain. Mum, tell him I want a second opinion.'

'We'll give you paracetamol,' said the doctor.

'Paracetamol?' I wasn't feeling reassured. I needed chocolate. I reached out with my good hand for the bar that Mum had bought.

'Enjoy that while you can,' said Dr Sam. 'If we're going to do you first thing, you'll need to starve from midnight tonight.'

'No breakfast?' I asked.

'Nope. And you won't be able to eat until after the operation either,' said the doctor.

I. Could. Not. Believe. It.

My fear began to change into a surge of rage as a nurse appeared with a hospital gown and I saw the last remnants of my dream life disappear. Mum took the gown from the nurse and I remembered the words of Dr Cronus when I'd said it was only a sprain. 'Don't bet on it,' he'd said. Grrr to you, whoever you are, I thought. Grrr, grrr, grrr! You can take your zodiac stuff, Dr Cronus, and you can take your ugly hospital gown, Dr Sam, and stick them up your bums. AAAAAArrrrrgh!

Chapter Six

Drama Queens

'I'll be back in the morning,' said Mum, after I was settled on my bed and the nurse had told her three times that she had to leave. Her eyes filled up with tears and she ignored all her requests to go even though the nurse was built like a heavyweight wrestler and Mum is a size eight. A badge on the nurse's uniform told us that her name was Abbie. She was so sweet with Mum, talking to her like she was about five and as if she were the one having to stay in hospital. I felt torn. Part of me wanted her to go so that I could get the attention I deserved, and part of me wanted her to stay because I didn't want to be alone in a strange place. The part that wanted her to go seemed to be winning. I felt miffed with her. I was the one in pain, the one whose life had been ruined, but she was acting as if it had all happened to her.

'I'm OK, Mum. You can go,' I said, but I still had my sulky face on. I couldn't help it. I had never felt so miserable. I had been motoring along nicely in the fast lane and now life had shoved a great big STOP sign on the road.

'You really have to leave now,' repeated Nurse Abbie. Her dark round face looked weary as if she had had a long day.

Mum stuck out her bottom lip and it wobbled as if she were about to burst into tears. 'Just another minute with my baby . . .'

'I'm not a baby. I'm twelve! Just go,' I blurted. 'I'll be fine.'

'Have you got any painkillers?' Mum asked the nurse.

'Oh, don't worry. We'll provide them for Marsha if she needs medication,' said Nurse Abbie.

'Not for her! For me,' said Mum, and the nurse gave her an exasperated look before walking away.

Mum wrapped me in an enormous hug, clinging on to me when I tried to pull away. 'Mum, just go. I will be OK, at least I probably will. Um . . . tell Dad – just in case anything goes wrong with my operation tomorrow – that I didn't mind that he didn't come to the hospital and felt it was more important to go to the pub with his rugby mates. He wasn't to know that it's as serious as it is.' (That will make him feel guilty, I thought. And I hope it does too!) 'And tell Cissie that if I die, she can have my DVDs – no, no, let Lois have them. And Eleanor can have my pink baseball cap, the one with Princess written on it. She's always wanted that.'

'Oh, don't talk like that. You know your dad would have been here,' Mum sobbed. 'I told him you'd just had a fall – I mean it's not the first time, is it? But it's never meant an operation before. Oh, oh, I can't leave you like this.'

'Yes. Yes, you can. Go on, back home, to my sisters, to your comfy bed. Oh, I do hope I see them again . . . yes, go . . . I'll be all right in this cold, strange place. I'll be fine.'

I put on my best heroic face at this point, but it only made Mum look more anxious.

'Oh, come on, Mum. It's not like I'm really going to die or anything, although . . . I have heard of people going into hospital and never coming out again.'

Mum let out an audible sob and I saw the girl in the bed to the left glance over. She looked as if she were about to burst out laughing. She was about my age and looked like an Afro princess lying propped up on pillows, pillows that didn't look like the lumpy hospital kind on my bed, and she was dressed in bright red silk PJs that most definitely weren't hospital issue. There appeared to be something wrong with her leg, because it was propped up by pillows under the blanket. I suddenly felt embarrassed for Mum carrying on. She could be such a drama queen!

'My darling baby,' she murmured into my hair. 'Your poor arm and your poor hair too.'

'Mu-um,' I groaned.

'Mrs Leibowitz,' called Nurse Abbie.

'Coming, coming, going, going,' Mum called back, and she finally let me go. She got up, sighed loudly à la tragic heroine, with the back of her hand on her forehead, made her way along the ward and at the end she stopped, turned, sighed again and flounced through the double doors, leaving them swinging in her wake.

I glanced over at the girl in the red PJs. She was staring at me.

'Nice performance,' she said.

I rolled my eyes to the ceiling. 'I know. She's always like that,' I said. 'So embarrassing.'

'Not her,' said the girl. 'You.'

'What do you mean? Me?'

The girl laughed. 'All that oh, I might die stuff, laying it on with a shovel.'

I felt outraged. 'Laying it on with a shovel? Er, excuse me, but you don't even know what happened to me.'

The girl shrugged. 'Yeah, I do. You broke or twisted your arm or something. I heard the nurses talking about it before you came up. Your poor mum. You were really making her suffer.'

'I-I—' I was lost for words. Hadn't she got eyes as well as ears? Couldn't she see my terrible dilemma? 'It's not just this you know. I was up to play the main part in the school show. All that's gone for a burton now, I bet. My whole life is ruined because of this . . .' I turned away. I didn't want to talk to her any more. She was obviously so wrapped up in herself that she didn't care about anyone else.

'You're not the only one whose life isn't working out. So get over it. At least you will. You'll recover. There are people in here who are really ill, you know.'

I turned back to look at her. 'Oh, sorry. I . . . er . . . are you very ill?'

'Not me. I'll recover too,' she said, then lowered her voice and jerked her chin towards someone in the third bed in our section. 'Amy down there.'

I couldn't see much of who was in that bed, just the top of someone's head, someone with brown hair. Oh God, there are sick people in here, I thought.

'What's the matter with her?' I whispered back to the girl but she had returned to her magazine as if she had lost interest in me. 'Oi, you,' I hissed.

The girl turned round. 'Skye,' she said. 'My name is Skye not Oi, you. You need to learn some manners, girl.'

'I . . .' I felt like someone had poured a bucket of cold water over me. I don't like you, I thought. 'And you need to learn to be more sensitive,' I said. 'This is my first time in hospital, you know, and although, OK, I might not be dying, I don't like it and I don't want to be here.'

Skye shrugged. 'Welcome to my world,' she said, before returning to her magazine. I decided not to ask what was wrong with Amy. In fact, I wouldn't talk to Skye at all if I could help it. Just because we were in the same ward didn't mean that we had to be friends.

I looked around at my surroundings properly. I hadn't had a chance when we'd first got up there because Dr Sam had been waiting for me and had swished the curtain round my bed while he hoisted my arm up into the air in the Bradford sling thing. I'd felt like a right banana when he'd finished. I would have to sit upright all night with my arm bound up in sky-blue spongy stuff and the whole contraption was strung up to a hook on the wall beside the bed.

'For your comfort,' he had said, but I couldn't get my head around that. Surely it would be way more comfy if I could lie down with my hand by my side? It felt cumbersome having it up in the air because I couldn't move it. This is how prisoners who are being tortured must feel, I thought, as I squirmed to get into a position that was comfortable. Only I haven't done anything bad.

From my vantage point, the ward appeared to be divided up into different sections. There were four beds in my bit, one of which was empty. I glanced down to Amy's bed, but still couldn't see her, and at that moment a female doctor walked past and pulled the curtains round her. I looked around at the rest of the ward. The walls were white, the curtains a bright turquoise and the lights overhead were really bright. I didn't like what was happening and I didn't want to be there. I wanted to be at home under my soft, cosy pink duvet surrounded by my things. A wave of anxiety came over me when I thought of what I was in for in the next few days. I had slept away from home before, loads of times, at camp or sleepovers, but never in a place like this. A place that was full of strangers and sharp steel instruments and the smell of disinfectant. Suddenly I wanted Mum back. It's only for a night, I told myself. You can do this. I blinked back sudden tears and hoped that no one had seen and thought that I was a weed.

'Hey, newbie,' called the Afro princess. 'What's your name?'

'Marsha,' I said, but I didn't look at her when I said it and I hoped she got the message that I didn't want to talk to her.

The noise of a trolley being wheeled into our section disturbed any conversation and the smell of boiled meat hit my nostrils.

'Dinner,' said Nurse Abbie. She bustled over to me, pushed a movable table over the bed and then plonked down a tray of food. A piece of meat with onions and some tinned sweet corn. It looked and smelt disgusting.

'No, thanks,' I said.

'Aren't you hungry?'

'Yes, but I'm not eating that.'

Nurse Abbie laughed. 'Can't say I blame you, darlin', but it's all you's a-gettin'.'

'Then I won't eat anything.'

'I'll leave it here a while,' said the nurse. 'You might change your mind later when you get hungry.'

She moved off towards Skye. I felt so frustrated. The smell of the food was making me feel nauseous but there was nothing I could do. I couldn't push it away, nor could I get up and walk away.

'Need some help?' asked Skye.

I made a face at the food. 'This smells disgusting,' I said.

Skye laughed. 'You're quite the princess, aren't you?'

'No,' I said. I objected to her insinuating that I was a princess, as if I were spoilt or something even though I had thought that she was a princess too. 'It's just that it smells horrible.'

'This isn't the Hilton, you know,' said Skye. 'So, unless you've got something tucked away, Abbie was right – that's all you're going to get.'

I shrugged and pushed the food away with my good hand. I must have overestimated the edge of the movable trolley, because the plate slipped and clattered to the floor, causing Nurse Abbie to jump.

'Oh, for heaven's sake,' said Skye. 'She's having a tantrum now.'

'No. I . . .' I wasn't having a tantrum. She so doesn't get me, I thought as Abbie came over and, letting out a weary sigh, began to pick up the mess. 'I'm sorry. I didn't mean to break it.' I felt tears prick the back of my eyes. I wanted my mum and my dad and Cissie and Eleanor and Lois. People who were on my side. An overwhelming feeling of frustration overtook me and I felt worried that I might start blubbing. I so didn't want to do that in case Skye saw and laughed again. She had clearly formed a bad opinion of me plus there was something about her that seemed very street and I didn't want her to think that I was uncool, a big baby, scared of being away from home.

The curtains round the third bed were pulled back and the nurse and doctor who had been in there came out. Their expressions were serious. I glanced over to try to see Amy but couldn't see much – still just a head with brown hair on the pillow. I wondered what her story was. I thought about asking Skye, but noticed that she had put her headphones on.

After a while, Nurse Abbie came and took the food away with another weary sigh. I thought about asking her about Amy, but by the way she brusquely cleared everything away I gauged that she wasn't in the mood for a chat. She positioned the small TV that was attached to the ceiling so that I could see it and she handed me the remote. After she'd gone, I flicked channels but there wasn't much on. In the end I watched a detective story just to pass the time.

At around ten, the lights went out. I heard Skye

snuggle down but Amy hadn't stirred at all.

'Night, newbie,' whispered Skye.

'My name's Marsha,' I whispered back.

'Night, newbie,' Skye whispered again. I didn't respond and after a while I could tell by her even breathing that she had fallen asleep.

Lucky thing, I thought. It was so weird sitting in my strange bed in the dark. I couldn't even lie down, put the covers over my head and pretend that I wasn't there. In my upright position, my eyes grew accustomed to the dark and the ward filled with shadows. Outside I could hear the drone of distant traffic. Inside all was quiet apart from the occasional sounds of footsteps, voices, a door opening or closing in the distance. I knew that I was in a hospital surrounded by people – doctors, nurses and patients – but I had never felt so alone in my whole life.

Chapter Seven

Op Day One

'Wargh!' I cried as I felt a presence next to me. I opened my eyes. I didn't know where I was. My eyes adjusted to the soft light of morning. It wasn't a dream. It was a living nightmare. Bright overhead lights came on, flooding light into every shadow and I realized that I was still on the ward.

My brain hurt. My arm hurt. My eyes hurt. And I needed to go to the loo.

'Just checking that you're OK there,' said a small blonde nurse with an Irish accent. I looked at her badge. It said that her name was Cheryl.

'I-I need to move. My arm feels numb and I need the loo.'

'I'll unhook you and you can go,' said the nurse.

It had been a horrible night. The whole time I could hear the nurses talking and laughing in their room down the corridor at the end of the ward and there were so many disturbances: lights going on and off, someone being brought in on a stretcher, lowered voices, strange beeps, moans, the sound of water dripping, machines clicking and someone (I suspected Skye) snoring. The thought of my lovely snuggly bed in my quiet room made me ache with homesickness. At last, however, I must have fallen into a light doze in the early hours because I wasn't aware of anything more until Cheryl had appeared.

'Won't be long now,' said Cheryl again. 'They'll come and get you soon, so they will.'

Great, I thought, the sooner the better, then I'm out of here. 'Soon when?'

'Maybe in about an hour.'

'An hour?' It sounded like such a long time.

Cheryl nodded and shoved some kind of contraption in my ear. It made me jump.

'What's that?'

'It takes your temperature,' she said, and then she put a black plastic armband round my arm. I knew from yesterday that it took my blood pressure.

'Can I have a cup of tea or some juice?' I asked when she'd finished.

Cheryl shook her head. 'Nothing until after the op.'

'So why did you wake me?'

'To check that you were all right.'

I groaned. 'I was all right. I was asleep. And now I'm not. So I'm not all right. Why didn't you just leave me?'

'It's my job to check on people in the morning.'

'That's so totally cruel. Surely the kindest thing would

be to let people sleep?'

Cheryl shrugged. 'Rules is rules, so they are.' She unhooked me so that I could go to the bathroom then she tottered off to poke Skye awake. She didn't seem too pleased about it either and groaned loudly. 'Leave me alone.'

I hobbled to the loo. My ankle was still sore, but not as bad as yesterday. When I came back into the ward, I saw Cheryl tiptoe over to Amy's bed and take her temperature. She didn't wake up. Lucky thing, I thought. She's dead to the world. And then I shuddered. She was lying very still. Ohmigod, maybe she is dead!

Skye had turned over and gone back to sleep. Cheryl hooked my arm back up, but I couldn't go back to sleep. I was wide awake. I saw that there was a remote control by the side of the bed that was labelled 'bed adjustor'. I decided to press a few of the buttons to see if it would make my bed more comfortable. I pressed on the controls with my good hand to see what it did. Legs up, legs down. Cool, I thought. Mattress up a bit, down a bit. Up, down, forward, back. And then my hand slipped and the bottom half of my bed began to rise. My legs went up and up – if I wasn't careful, I was going to fold in two.

'Oooooo whoaaaa, Nurse!' I cried.

Cheryl was there in an instant and I could see that she was having a hard time not laughing.

'It's not funny,' I said. I felt close to tears again. I was really thirsty. 'How long before they come to get me?'

Cheryl checked her watch. 'Forty-five minutes or so,' she said, and she scurried off back down the ward.

I groaned again.

'Be quiet, newbie,' Skye called from her bed. 'Some of us are trying to get some kip here.'

'And some of us are trying to find something to do. It's so boring in here,' I said, and kicked off the sheets. 'And so hot.'

In reply, Skye put a pillow over her head. Soon after, she got out of bed and hobbled down the ward with her toilet bag, so I presumed that she was going to the bathroom.

While she was gone, Cheryl came over and said that my mobile had bleeped. Someone had been trying to get through.

'My mum,' I said.

'No. He said he was your guardian.'

Must be Dad, I thought, and about time. 'But I thought that we couldn't use our mobiles in here.'

'You can text and occasionally take a call,' said Cheryl. 'Do you want me to get it for you?'

I nodded and Cheryl rooted around in my drawer. She pulled out the zodiac phone and was about to hand it to me.

'Not that one. The silver one,' I said. 'I won that one. I don't even know if it works.'

Cheryl looked back in the drawer then handed me both

phones. 'Yes, it does. It was this red phone that was bleeping, but you can see if you have any messages on either.'

I looked on the screen of my usual phone. There was one message, but it wasn't from Dad. It was a text from Lois.

Ohmigod. Wl cm 2 C U l8r. Lois. XXXXX.

I checked again to see if I had missed the one from Dad but there was definitely nothing else on there. I looked on my zodiac phone. I pressed what seemed like the ON button on the keypad and seconds later, it bleeped that I had a message. I found the message section and read:

Zodiac Girl. Yours is the sign of the warrior. You are ruled by Mars, god of war. My message to you is be brave. Keep fighting. I will be in touch. Your guardian, Mario Ares, aka Mars.

Wow, I thought. That's kind of curious. How could he have known what happened to me? Maybe he didn't. Not really. Maybe it's a random message that they send out to all Aries girls? Yeah. I guess that's it. You could tell anyone to keep fighting and it would probably apply to their situation. Whatever. It's still a cool phone.

As I played around with the buttons, I noticed that there

were already ten numbers in the address book. I scrolled down.

Mr O: the sun

Selene: the moon

Hermie: Mercury

Nessa: Venus

PJ: Pluto

Joe: Jupiter

Mario: Mars

John Dory: Neptune

Dr Cronus: Saturn. That batty old man from the waiting room, I realized.

Uri: Uranus. Uri Uranus? I asked myself. Wasn't he the man on the unicycle who waited with me after I'd fallen? His name was Uri, wasn't it? Hmm. Weird.

As I was wondering about the names, a dark young man with dreadlocks, wearing a green overall, came through the double doors with what looked like the breakfast trolley. He went from section to section and when he got to ours Amy was still asleep, but Skye sat up and chose Weetabix and toast.

'Only things they can't ruin,' she said, and tucked in moments later.

'What are you in for?' I asked.

Skye shrugged. 'They found an alien living in my stomach.'

I laughed.

She didn't. Her expression was deadly serious.

'Oh . . . I . . .' I had a momentary panic that maybe it was some kind of rare disease, but then she pointed at her right foot under the bedclothes. With effort, she poked it out from under the covers and I could see that it was in plaster.

'Duh. My ankle,' she said. She turned back to her cereal as if to say that was the end of that conversation.

After breakfast, the nurses seemed to go into overdrive. I couldn't see much from where I was, but I could hear the activity. All the time, there hadn't been a peep out of Amy in the third bed.

'Is that girl all right?' I asked Cheryl as she approached my bed with a bald male nurse in a green gown.

Cheryl breathed out heavily. 'Not sure, not sure. Oh, and here's Jacob to wheel you down.'

Jacob gave me a friendly smile and all further questions about Amy went out of the window as I thought, At last. Now, I can get this thing over with and get out of here. I sat up and even though I wasn't looking forward to what they were going to do I put on my best brave face. 'I'm ready,' I said. 'Do your worst.'

Jacob smiled again. 'I am sorry,' he said. 'But we have had a number of emergencies. An accident out on the motorway – a pile-up – and there have been several cases brought in that are urgent.'

'Er, well, thanks for the news flash, but what has that

got to do with me?'

'We'll have to delay your op until tomorrow,' he said.

'Delay? Nooo, but . . . I've been waiting all night.'

'I know, and we're sorry, but in these cases, we have to prioritize,' he said, and began to back out of the ward. 'Got to dash.'

'Noooooo. But . . . what about MEEEEEEE?' I called after him.

Cheryl smiled. 'Well, at least you can have a cup of tea. Will I bring you a cup and some toast, then?'

'No. I'll go home and wait there,' I said.

'I don't think the doctors will let that happen,' said Nurse Cheryl. 'Oh no, not likely.' She bustled off down the ward.

I felt like throwing something at someone. Normally I am not a tantrum sort of person but I felt indignant. Didn't anyone realize that I had spent the whole night sitting up, starving and uncomfortable? This. Couldn't. Be. Happening.

'I DON'T WANT ANYTHING!' I shouted, causing Skye to glance over and raise an eyebrow. 'And you can stop staring at me.' She shrugged her shoulders as if to say, whatever.

It so wasn't fair. If I'd felt miserable last night when I'd come in, it was nothing to how I felt now. Another day in this brightly lit hell hole? I couldn't bear it. 'CHERYL!'

She turned back. 'What is it now?'

'I am so uncomfortable. Can't you unhook me for a while, please? I can't bear sitting here like this.'

'I can put you in a high arm sling for a while if you like but only for a while because the Bradford sling helps to reduce the swelling. And don't shout like that. You'll scare the other patients.'

I don't care, I thought, but when I glanced over at Amy's bed I saw that she had woken up and was looking around like a startled mouse and then I did feel a bit mean. At least I'll be getting out of here soon; she looks like she's in for a long while. She looked over at me and I gave her a little wave with my good hand, and smiled. She looked like she could do with a friend.

After a short while, Cheryl brought me some breakfast, white toast and jam.

'I don't eat white bread,' I said. 'Haven't you got wholegrain?'

Cheryl laughed. 'Ah, you're a one, so you are,' she said, and she left the plate of toast on the table that could be moved across the bed.

I manoeuvred myself the best I could in order to eat it and, actually, it wasn't too bad. Skye was right. It would be hard to ruin toast and the cup of tea was wonderful after not being able to drink for so long.

After breakfast, I watched people come and go. Dad rang at around ten and I filled him in on what had happened.

'Oh,' he said. 'Your mother rang the hospital first thing

and they said you were first on the list to go down to the theatre.'

'Change of plan. There was an accident and now I'm last on the list. Dad, can't I go private? Can't you do something about this? Surely you know someone who knows someone. I'm in agony. Or at least get me out of here for today. There's no point in staying here like this.'

'I'll come in later with your mother,' said Dad. 'Sit tight and I'll see what I can do.'

'Don't be long. It's like time has slowed down in here.'

After Dad's call, I had another look at the zodiac phone. As I was playing with it, it bleeped that I had another text message.

Give me a call when you need some entertaining. Uri

That would be nice, I thought, he seemed like a kind man, if a little eccentric. Some entertainment would be great.

I decided to leave a message and send it to all of the names in the address book and see what happened. There was nothing else to do, it would pass the time and I had nothing to lose.

I wrote my message.

Zodiac Girl in need of help. In hospital. Needs supplies, entertainment, pampering. Urgent. SOS

Then I pressed SEND TO ALL. OK, I said to myself, let's see if this zodiac thing really is a prize worth having!

As I put the phone back in the drawer next to the bed, I noticed Skye watching me. 'What've you got there?' she asked.

'Just a mobile phone,' I said. 'I won it on the Internet. It's supposed to be a zodiac phone, but I'm not really sure what it does yet.'

She got out of her bed, hobbled over and sat on the edge of mine. I gave her the phone to look at.

'It's a cool phone,' she said as she turned it over. 'Stylish.'

'Thanks,' I said. I was about to ask her more about her leg when the staff nurse came over and asked Skye to go back to her bed so that her doctor could see her. Minutes later, the double doors at the end of the ward opened and the doctor appeared. He went to Skye's bed and swished the curtains closed. I did my best to hear what he was saying, but couldn't catch many words.

After he'd gone Skye seemed subdued. When I glanced over, she was lying with her eyes open, looking up at the ceiling. I glanced further along the ward. Amy was also awake. She too was lying on her back staring at the ceiling. If I'd been able to move, I might have got out of my bed and gone to talk to her, but I was still fastened to the wall with my spongy blue handcuff and I didn't want to do any more damage to my arm by unhooking it myself. Ah, happy days, NOT, I thought as I glanced at my watch. It was only eight o'clock. I looked up at the ceiling to see what it was that was so fascinating up there to the others.

Big white ceiling tiles.

A long fluorescent light tube.

A bit of pink balloon material in the far right of the ceiling. I wonder how that got up there.

I looked around the ward.

And back up at the ceiling.

And back around the ward.

I looked at my watch. It was ten past eight.

Bug bottoms. I AM SO BORED, I thought. It's like time has stopped. In all my life, I don't think I have sat still for so long. Aaargh. No. No. OK. I can do this. I'm an Aries and, as Mario said, we are fighters. I'm not a giver in. I've never admitted defeat about anything in my life. I just have to get the right attitude. Yogis and guru-type people do it when they meditate in remote caves in India. I've seen them on the telly. They don't have anything to distract them. No radio, no movies, no nothing. And they find peace. Maybe I'll come out of here totally enlightened. Maybe I'll just float out of here. Saint Marsha. Swami Marsha. That will be me. Oh . . . I wish that there was something to do. I don't think Skye looks like she wants to chat just now. And Amy, she looks really ill. I wonder if it's catching. Oh God, I hope not. Poor thing. When I can move, I'll try to cheer her up. I wonder if she feels lonely in here too. It's weird being away from home and not knowing what's going to happen. Oh, it's SO boring here. I'll see if I catch the nurse's attention. She keeps walking past, always in a hurry, never makes eye contact. Oh Gee-od, I wish something would happen. So much for being a Zodiac Girl. Since I got that news, everything has gone wrong. And nothing's happened since I sent out my cry for help to zodiac people.

An hour later and still no one had come.

Another hour and still no one.

Just nurses, cleaners, the occasional doctor, a lady with a tea trolley. No exciting zodiac people, that was for sure.

At last it was visiting hour and I waited in anticipation for the nurses to open the doors. Mum was first through and came bustling in, laden down with promising-looking bags. I had never been so glad to see her in all of my life, not even after the summer camp when I was nine when it had rained nonstop and everyone had got a stomach bug and been utterly miserable. Mum had brought lots of goodies and a card that Lois had dropped around that morning. In the bags were magazines, fruit, chocolate, a toilet bag, my sky-blue pyjamas and a few books.

'I've had an awful night,' she said (like I hadn't), 'but I've come through it and decided that I have to be brave. Be positive.'

'Good for you,' I said sarcastically, but she didn't seem to get it.

'Yes, isn't it?' she replied. 'I have to be strong. For you, love.'

'Where's Dad?'

'Parking the car,' she replied, and, indeed, he did appear about five minutes later. I felt a lump in my throat seeing his familiar round face and when he gave me a hug I breathed in his safe 'Dad' smell of lemon aftershave mixed with pencil shavings. He was dressed in his weekend casuals of jeans and a fleece, and his dark hair, which was usually neatly combed back for the office on weekdays, flopped over his forehead.

'You have to get me out of here,' I said. 'Can I go private?'

Dad chuckled. 'I've had a word with the doctor and you're in the best possible hands here. Chin up. Be my brave girl.'

Chin up? Brave girl? He clearly had no idea. I decided not to speak to him for the rest of the visit. Not that he noticed. He ate my grapes and read my magazine like it was enough that he'd simply shown up. I could not believe it. And Mum was jabbering about what was on telly, what was in the paper, what and who she'd seen on the way up to the ward. What had happened to the tearful Mum of last night? She seemed to have had a personality change and was being brusque and breezy. It was very annoying.

Luckily, the things she left were enough to pass the time until the second visiting hour in the early evening and this time Lois came back with her. She too had brought me presents. A magazine, a loan of her fluffy pink pig toy (which was sweet because I knew that she had slept with him since she was three years old, so it was a big thing for her to let him go for a night). I was touched by that, I really was, but I also felt annoyed with her. And Mum. They both put on drippy faces, like they were so sorry for me, and talked to me like I had lost my brain.

'There will be other shows,' said Lois, and she patted my good hand.

I pulled my hand back. 'No, there won't,' I replied. 'Not other shows with Ollie—'

'Swoon, swoon,' said Lois.

I rolled my eyes. I didn't feel like saying the 'swoon, swoon' like we always did. 'As I was saying, not with Ollie or his dad. It was my one big chance.'

'There will be other opportunities,' said Mum in a sugary voice. 'You're still young.'

Lois nodded. 'You're still young. You've got your whole life ahead of you.'

'No! You don't understand,' I said. I couldn't believe that Lois was coming out with the same rubbish as Mum. If anyone ought to have understood, it was her, but she clearly didn't. I saw Skye glance over. She had an amused look in her eye. I stuck my tongue out at her. I felt cross. Cross with everyone. I couldn't help it and even though there was a part of me that was telling myself not to be a strop queen, I couldn't pull myself out of it. It felt like I had sinking sand around me and I was being sucked down into it.

I glanced over at Skye again. She had a lot of visitors around her bed. I did a quick count. Six. Two big ladies, two middle-aged men who were probably their husbands and a boy and girl who looked in their twenties. Relatives, by the looks of them, and they were having a merry old time, gossiping and eating the food that they'd brought in. It must be something all visitors do, I thought as I watched Lois pop another of my grapes into her mouth. Amy only had one visitor, a tall pale lady who looked like her mum. They were very quiet and sat in silence, holding hands and watching the rest of us for most of the hour. There was something about Amy that looked so sad; my heart went out to her.

When the evening visiting time was over and all the visitors had gone apart from mine, I felt so envious of Mum and Lois being able to get up and walk out.

'Please don't leave me here,' I begged, and I put on my best I am in agony face. 'Please. I hate it in here. You don't know how awful it is and how much pain I'm in.' I let out a groan and a sob. If that doesn't get me out of here, I don't know what will, I thought as Lois looked at me anxiously. 'Ooo, oooo, ahhhh, ooch, ooch.'

Sadly, Mum really did seem to have had a personality change since last night, like someone had flipped a switch in her and she had gone into her 'we must be strong' persona. 'Darling, it's only for one more night,' she said, and then she went into a lispie little-girlie voice. 'Be my big gwown up girl and show us all how bwave you can be.'

Bog right off, I thought.

'It's all right for you,' I said. 'And you, Lois. You can go back to your homes, with fridges full of food and beds with comfy pillows, while I have to stay here and suffer.'

This time, Skye did laugh, and out loud too.

'And you can shut up,' I called across to her.

Mum looked shocked. 'Marsha. That's not like you. You must be nice to the other girls in here.' She turned to Skye. 'I must apologize for my daughter. She's not herself.'

Skye gave Mum a winning smile. 'No probs. It can be hard for the younger ones being away from their mums and dads.'

'Thank you, dear,' said Mum, and turned back to me. 'What a charming girl.'

Behind Mum, Skye stuck her tongue out at me.

I hate you, I thought as Mum and Lois walked towards the double doors and the exit and freedom. I hate everyone.

To my left, Skye chuckled softly.

I wanted to kill her.

Chapter Eight

Op Day Two

Oh, noooooo, I thought when I awoke the following day to find that I was still in the ward. I had been dreaming that I was at home in my own bed. Nurse Cheryl took my blood pressure and my temperature and the bright ceiling lights came on, flooding the ward with unnatural light. This is like that film *Groundhog Day*, where the main character keeps reliving the same day, I thought as I watched the ward staff go into the same routines as yesterday and patients begin to stir in their beds.

Luckily, I didn't have to wait long this time before Jacob arrived in his green gown. 'First on the list today, Marsha,' he said. 'It will all be over before you know it. Ready for a little ride?'

I gave him a weak smile back and tried not to let the feeling of fear overtake me as the nurses got me ready. It will be OK, I told myself. I'm glad it's happening at last because the sooner we do it the sooner I'll be out of here and back where I belong.

Fifteen minutes later, I was on a trolley being wheeled

through brightly lit corridors. Part of me felt like sitting up, leaping off the trolley and doing a runner but another more sensible part knew there was no getting out of it. Once in the anaesthetist's room, a big smiley man, also in a green hospital gown, fussed around. Dr Sam made a brief appearance and touched my foot as if to say, don't worry, I'm here, but I wasn't reassured. The urge to get up and run for it was still there. Too late, I realized as the big smiley man came at me with a needle.

'This won't hurt,' he said as he put it in my arm. 'You'll have a sensation of cold and then you'll go to sleep and it will all be over.'

I felt the prick of the needle and waited for the sensation. I can't feel the cold, I thought. It's not working. It's NOT WORKING! I'm going to be awake all the way through the operation. Oh, no . . . oooo. Zzzzzzzzzzzzzzzzzzzzzzzzzzzzzzzzzzzzzzzzzzzzzzzzzzzzz . . .

I woke some time later. I was back in the ward. It was all over and Mum was next to my bed and my arm was in a sling tucked down by my side. After a slight hiccup (I felt groggy when I came round and threw up all over Mum!), I was allowed a cup of tea and some toast and not long after, I began to feel a little nauseous but almost back to normal.

'How does the wrist feel?' Mum asked.

I focused on the area where it had been fractured. 'Better, actually. That is, it's a little sore but it feels OK and at least I don't have to sit upright any more. I can't tell you how heavenly it feels to be able to lie down! When do I get out?'

'Soon,' said Mum. 'I think the nurse said that Dr Heaton wanted to do another X-ray and check in on you afterwards and then you can probably go home later today.'

'Phew. Nightmare almost over,' I said. 'What time exactly?'

'Around three, he said.'

After the morning visitors, the ward seemed quiet again. I got up and found the bathroom and clumsily brushed my teeth with my good hand. Soon I'll be free, I said to my reflection. I did look odd. Being away from mirrors, I'd forgotten that my hair was white plus now that the gel had worn off, I could see that the bleach had made it very dry. And it itched. Mum had tied it back neatly for me when she'd been in but I was longing to give it a good wash. 'You've got hair like straw, m'dear,' I said to myself in the mirror.

When I went back to bed, I looked at the clock. Eleven. Four more hours, I thought. I did my best to keep occupied with my books and magazines, but I was grateful when a nurse came to take me for the X-ray as that made the time go even faster.

When I got back to the ward, Skye was reading and Amy was sleeping, but they were no longer my concern. In a few hours they, along with this ward, would be history.

One o'clock came round. One five. One ten. One fifteen. I read a little. One and three quarter hours to go, I told myself. Can't wait. Can't wait. I watched TV for a while, but when I looked at the clock again it seemed like only seconds had gone by. Time in hospital really does go slower than anywhere else on the planet, I thought, looking at the clock again. One forty.

When Dr Sam came to check on me, I was sitting up trying to look as well as I could and I had my regular mobile ready to call Mum to let her know that she could come to get me. Please, please, please let me go home this afternoon, I thought as he approached the bed.

He asked me a few questions about my wrist and how I felt.

'Great. I feel great. Thanks for everything. Now can I go home?'

Dr Sam grimaced. 'Didn't the ward sister tell you?'

My stomach tightened into a knot. 'Tell me what?'

'About the X-ray machine?'

'No. Why? What? Is there something still wrong with my wrist?'

'No. No, nothing like that,' said Dr Sam. 'It's just that

we're having problems with the X-ray machine and we couldn't get a clear picture.'

'But haven't you got another machine?'

Dr Sam nodded. 'We do, but they're all busy. The queues have been waiting here for hours. People wait for months for their appointments.'

'So when can I do it again?'

'Hopefully in the morning. The technicians are looking at it now, but, even if it gets fixed today, we have to wait our turn for it and the emergency cases always take precedence. You shouldn't have to be here too long. You'll just have to stay in another night.'

'Wha—? Another night? Again? No. Please. Can't I go home and then come back tomorrow?'

Dr Sam shook his head. 'With your kind of injury, there's a slight risk of swelling. We need to keep you where we can keep an eye on it until we're a hundred per cent certain.'

'But—'

'Be a couple of days tops. It's for your own good.'

'Couple of days? You just said one more night.' The nightmare was getting worse and worse.

Dr Sam shrugged. 'You can never be too sure. I hope it will be tomorrow, but it depends on what the problem with the machine is.'

I could feel something in the pit of my stomach, like a churning volcano, burning, burning, ERUPTING into a noise in my throat. 'NOOOOOOOO. Please. Let me go home, please.'

Dr Sam shook his head. 'Come on now. It's not that bad,' he said, then his bleeper went and he began to move towards the doors giving me a cheery wave as he went.

I. Could. Not. Believe. It!

'This so isn't fair,' I called after him.

But he was gone and so were my hopes of freedom.

Chapter Nine

Mr Mars

Two o'clock.

Three o'clock.

Three fifteen.

Three twenty.

Three twenty-five.

What was going on with the clock? Surely time couldn't be going so slowly?

At four, Mum arrived for the afternoon visiting hour and I saw the nurses explain the situation to her.

'Oh, darling, I am sorry. I did call and they told me, which is why I didn't come earlier,' she said when she came over to my bed. 'But it won't be long. Only another day or so.'

'Another day or so? You just don't understand. Something has happened to time in here,' I said. 'It has slowed down. It's like being stuck in a time warp that never moves on.'

A flicker of a smile crossed Mum's face.

'What?' I asked. 'What's funny?'

'Nothing, darling, just . . . it was the way you put that. It was cute. Stuck in a time warp.'

I didn't feel cute. I decided that it was her fault. All of it. The fall. The X-ray machine. All of it. And I wasn't going to speak to her apart from to ask two questions.

'Is Lois coming in later?'

Mum shook her head. 'She has a rehearsal for the school show.'

My stomach sank. I felt so jealous. I would have been doing my own rehearsals tomorrow night. With Ollie. The thought of it all happening without me made me feel like crying.

'What about Cissie and Eleanor? Are either of them coming in?'

'No, darling. They thought you'd be out tonight and would see you at home.'

'Oh, did they? Well, you can go now. Seeing as none of you appear to really care, you may as well stop this pretence.'

Mum put her hand on my bandaged wrist. 'Ow!' I winced. It didn't actually hurt, but I wanted her to suffer too.

'Oh, Marsha, I am sorry. Does it hurt a lot?'

I glanced over at Skye to make sure that she wasn't watching me with her amused look, but she was busy with her own visitor, one of the ladies from Sunday who I reckoned was her mum. I nodded. 'It hurts more than you will ever know,' I said, and I stuck my bottom lip out. At the back of my mind, I could hear an inner voice say, You are acting like such a precious princess, Marsha Leibowitz. Get over yourself. But I couldn't help it. I felt utterly miserable. I didn't like where I was. I didn't like what had happened to me. And I didn't like the misery guts person I was becoming.

After Mum had gone, I looked over at Skye, but she seemed oblivious to her surroundings and had her iPod headphones on. I glanced further down the ward to see if Amy was awake, but her bed was empty. She must have got up when Mum was here and I didn't notice, I thought. I reached into the drawer in the cabinet next to me and texted Lois to tell her how unfair everything was. My zodiac phone was lying there. I picked that up. Just looking at it made me cross. I'd sent out a cry for help and there hadn't even been one reply. So much for it being a good prize, I thought as I picked it up and hurled it to the bottom of my bed. Unfortunately, I misjudged the distance and it almost hit Amy as she went past before it clattered to the floor. She leaped back in surprise then looked over at me. She bent over, picked it up and brought it over to me.

'I am so sorry,' I said. 'I didn't mean to give you a fright.'

She smiled and sat on the edge of my bed. 'That's OK. I'm Amy by the way.'

'Marsha.'

'You feeling mad about something?' Up close, I could see how pretty she was, with delicate features and big cornflower-blue eyes in a pale face. However, the purple shadows under her eyes, like bruises, showed that she wasn't well.

I nodded. 'And some. I just heard that I can't go home today and well . . . I was just letting off some steam. Sorry. Mum's always telling me that I act before I think and it should be the other way round.'

'I know how you feel,' she said. 'I was mad when I first came in here. It seemed so unfair, like, why me? You should have seen me. I was Queen of Tantrums.'

I smiled. She looked so pale and weak it was hard to imagine her having the energy to have a tantrum.

'But you get your head round it,' she continued. 'I guess I've got more used to it now and it's not so bad really.'

'What's the matter?' I asked, then I put my hand over my mouth. 'Oops. Sorry. Me and my big mouth. Not my business.'

'I don't mind. I have a type of Hodgkins disease. Something to do with my lymph glands.'

'Well, I hope you get better,' I said.

She gave me a sad smile. 'So do I. There are different kinds of it. It is treatable, but . . . oh never mind,' she said, then sighed. 'It's so boring talking about it.'

I glanced over at Skye who still had her headphones on. 'What's she in for?'

'She hurt her ankle. They had to put a pin in it.'

'Ooch,' I said. 'That sounds painful.'

Amy nodded. 'Yeah. She was pretty fed up about it too. Apparently she's a dancer—'

'A dancer? Really? So am I. Well, it's one of the things I do. I was supposed to be in the school show. I had the lead role.'

'Skye does hip hop. Apparently she was quite a star. All set to go through to some competition until she hurt her leg. I think she was very disappointed. Anyway, better get back to bed. I can't seem to stay up for long these days.'

'Give me the nod when you want some company,' I said. 'I'll come over for a chat.'

'That would be nice,' said Amy, who then went back to her bed.

I glanced over at Skye. We had more in common than I'd realized. It was a shame she was so stand-offish. I turned my attention back to Amy, climbing back into her bed. I wished there was something I could do to help. Maybe when I am out, I thought, I can send her something to cheer her up.

I sat and read magazines for a short while and tried to resist looking at the clock every five minutes. It was difficult. It kept pulling me like a magnet, then mocking me, like look at me, look at me. Ha ha. I've hardly moved on at all!

I decided to try my zodiac phone again. Why not? I thought. I have nothing to lose. I texted in:

When I said I needed help, I meant now. Zodiac Girl

The reply was instantaneous.

Chill out, Zodiac Girl. Your Mars is conjunct with the moon. We will be there soon. Keep fighting. Mario

Not long after, the doors to the ward opened and in walked Mr Ares and a lady who definitely didn't look like one of the nurses. She looked like . . . a mermaid on legs. She was tall and willowy with silver grey hair in a plait down her back and she was dressed like a Victorian governess in a long silver skirt and high neck jacket. Both of them seemed to know the nurses and as they talked they glanced over at me. They looked out of place in the hospital because they radiated light and health. Both Amy and Skye looked up to see Mario as he came over to see me.

He sat on the end of the bed. 'So. Marsha. What's all this nonsense?'

'What nonsense?'

'I think you know what I'm talking about.'

'No, I don't.'

'You haven't stopped moaning since you got in here.'

'Me. Wha—? But . . . in case you don't know, I have had an operation on my arm and have been confined to bed. Wouldn't that make most people moan?'

'Some people, yes, but not someone with a chart like yours and not someone who has been chosen to be a Zodiac Girl.'

'Oh that.'

'You have your phone and your pendant?'

'Yes. I won them as a prize.'

Mario shook his head. 'A prize? A PRIZE? You haven't got it, have you? It's a lot more than a prize.'

'What do you mean?'

'To be a Zodiac Girl means that you're a very lucky girl.'

I looked down at my arm. 'Lucky? Hah! Doesn't seem very lucky to me. In fact, life has been rubbish since I heard about the Zodiac Girl thing.'

'Well, it is lucky,' said Mario. 'Every month, somewhere on the planet, one girl is chosen to be a Zodiac Girl. Only one girl. She gets three things. A piece of jewellery. You got that, yeah?'

'My pendant with the little ram on it.'

'That would be it. She also gets introduced to her guardian, who is me. Me because you're an Aries. Each birth sign has a ruling planet. Mars rules Aries, so you get me.'

84

'Er, could you rewind the tape a mo?' I said. 'I get the ruling planet bit. But what have you, the person Mario, got to do with the planet Mars?'

'All the planets are here in human form. I am the living embodiment of Mars.'

I burst out laughing. 'Yeah, and I'm Queen Nefertiti.'

Mario looked offended. 'No, you're not. You're Marsha Leibowitz. I know it's a lot to get your head around, but it's true. We all live locally.'

'The planets all live locally?'

'Yeah.'

'And are here in human form?'

'Yeah.'

'OK . . .' He is clearly barking mad, I thought. He is in the hospital to see someone in the psychiatric unit and wandered in here by mistake. 'Um, just got to go to the loo.'

I hopped out of bed and limped over to the nurses' room. 'Hey, Cheryl, can I have a word?' I asked when I saw her sitting having a cup of tea with the lady that Mario had come in with.

'Sure. What is it?'

I beckoned her to come to the door so that the lady wouldn't hear.

'That man by the bed. I think he may have wandered out of the mental unit,' I whispered into her ear.

Cheryl laughed. 'No. That's Mario. There's no one

saner. He does physiotherapy here with some of the patients. But the lady I'm having a cuppa with, she's from the psychiatric unit. She's one of the counsellors. She visits all the teen wards once or twice a week.'

The lady behind waved. 'Hi, Marsha. I'm Selene. Cheryl's been telling me all about you.'

'Um . . . hi. Um . . . good.'

'Marsha,' called Mario. 'I haven't finished with you yet!'

I pinched myself as I went back to the bed. Maybe it was me that was going mad, either that or I was still asleep and having a very weird dream.

'So, Marsha,' Mario continued, 'I came in today to tell you that you have to change your attitude. Stop feeling sorry for yourself and have a good hard think about what is happening to you this month.'

'Easy. I can tell you exactly what's happening. I am having a rotten time. All my plans have been ruined.'

Mario put his hand to his mouth and yawned. 'Zodiac Girl, get over it. You're bigger than that and you're stronger than that. I am very disappointed to see you behaving like this.'

'So how should I be behaving?'

'Like a warrior. Like a leader. Don't you know that Aries is the first sign of the zodiac? People born under your sign become leaders, the movers and shakers of this world. Aries people don't give in, not without a fight.'

Although I was indignant that he didn't get how awful

my life was at present, a part of me felt like he was speaking to another part of me – a deeper, stronger part – and I couldn't help but respond. I wasn't going to let him know that, though. 'Whatever.'

'Fine. If that's your attitude, I'm leaving. For each Zodiac Girl it is different. Some use their gift, others ignore it, but remember this: we're here to help.'

'Yeah. Planets in human form,' I said, and put the finger of my good hand up to my temple and made a circle sign as if to say, you're living in lala land. He turned to walk away. I watched him go back into the room with Nurse Cheryl and Selene. I bet they're talking about me now, I thought as I saw them get into an animated conversation and Selene glanced over at our section. When I saw Mario sit down, I crept out of bed and then, making sure that I was out of their sight, I positioned myself so I could hear what they were saying, whilst to anyone in the ward I looked as if I were casually looking at some of the leaflets on display.

'Does she know?' asked Selene.

'I think she has some idea,' said Nurse Cheryl, 'but I don't think she realizes what a rough ride she's in for.'

'What are her chances?' asked Mario.

'We're not sure. We're keeping her in for longer while we do some further tests,' said Nurse Cheryl.

'Very sad,' said Mario. 'Poor thing. She has to keep fighting.'

My blood ran cold. Oh. My. God, I thought. They're talking about me. It's worse than I thought. I'm dying. I have to keep fighting. So that's why Mario came to deliver that little speech.

I felt faint. I need to get back to my bed if I haven't long to live, I thought, scuttling back towards my area before they caught me eavesdropping. Ohmigod. I wonder if Mum knows. I wonder how long I've got.

Chapter Ten

Selene

I felt numb. Outraged. In shock. One minute I was looking forward to playing the lead role in the school play. My whole life in front of me. Then what seemed a minor accident and my life is over? Over before it had even begun? It can't be. There are so many things I want to do. Travel the world. Be a famous actress. Have a boyfriend. I haven't even been snogged yet! I can't die before my first kiss! Preferably with Ollie Blake. Tears filled my eyes. I had been looking forward to going home. Counting the hours. Now maybe I will never see our house again.

Do Mum and Dad know? I wondered. And Lois? Oh, my dear friend. Who will she hang out with at the weekend? Who will she talk to? In my mind's eye, I could see Lois sitting on her own in the school playground. Her face pale. No one to share her lunch with. No one to have a laugh with. No one to gossip with about what was on telly. About who we fancied. Ollie. No one to say 'swoon, swoon' with. She'd be lonely without me.

And not just her.

I could see the dining table at home. Mum and Dad, Cissie and Eleanor and a place set for me. An empty place. An empty chair. No one would be able to eat, they'd be so choked, so sad. And my funeral. A coffin covered in white roses and yellow freesias. Or red roses and ivy? Hmm. I'll decide later. But all the school will be there. Heads bowed. Someone would probably get a video together of the highlights of my life: when I won the badminton tournament. When I was nine and the Swan Queen in the Swan Lake ballet. When I played Joseph in the nativity play in junior school. It would be so moving for everyone to watch.

What music should I have? Something light-hearted to remind people of some aspect of my character and make them smile? Or something sad with loads of violins to make them cry buckets? Who would get up to talk about me? Dad? Mrs Pierson? Lois? Not Lois. She wouldn't be able to get any words out she'd be so gutted. It was making me cry just thinking about it. Cut off in her prime, everyone would say. She had everything to live for. She was going to be somebody, that one, but all the good ones die young, don't they? Tears spilled out on to my cheeks at the thought of how moving it would be.

Mario and Selene came out of the nurse's office. I saw Mario look in the direction of my area, and he said something to Selene. She nodded, then he left and she came over. She looked amazing, with sea-green eyes in a pale face and the air of someone from a fantasy book about fairies or mermaids.

'Hi there, Marsha. So how are you feeling?' Selene asked.

'Pretty awful. Numb really.'

Selene looked at my wrist. 'Numb? Don't worry. The feeling will come back.'

'I guess,' I said. 'It's just I . . . I can't take it in. It doesn't seem fair. I'm trying to get my head round what's happened, but it doesn't seem real.'

'Yes. A lot of girls say that when they find out,' said Selene.

'Do they? Oh . . .' I didn't know whether to let on that I knew how bad things were because she'd know that I'd been eavesdropping, but I decided why not. If I only had limited time, I may as well be as honest as I could for what was left of it. 'Um. I know you know.'

Selene smiled. 'Of course I know. And I know you know.'

I wasn't sure that she got it. 'No. I mean I know . . .'

'And I know you know,' said Selene.

'So you know that I know that you know?'

Selene looked slightly puzzled. 'Yes. Of course. Um . . . what are we talking about?'

'About me.'

'Being Zodiac Girl, yes?' asked Selene.

'No. That I'm going to die.'

'Die?' asked Selene, and she sat on the end of the bed. 'Oh that.'

'Yes. That. So it's true?' A feeling of horror took me over as Selene nodded. I'd been half hoping that she was going to tell me that it was all a terrible mistake.

'Well, we're all going to die, aren't we?' said Selene. 'There's no avoiding it. One thing is for certain and that is that we all have to go sometime, but not many girls your age think about it. Most girls your age think they are invincible.'

'Ah, but I know that I'm not.'

'Well, that makes you a very wise person, Marsha.'

'Only because I know.'

Selene looked slightly confused. 'Yes, you know. Marsha, er . . . what exactly is it you think you know?'

I leant towards her so that the others wouldn't hear. 'That my injury is worse than anyone thought. That I may not have long.'

'And what makes you think that?'

'I . . . I heard you talking in . . .' I pointed at the staff room.

'Ah.' Selene nodded. 'You heard us talking.' Then she laughed. I was shocked. She's a rubbish counsellor if she laughs at dying patients, I thought.

'You're not being very sympathetic, whoever you are. Are you properly qualified?' I asked.

'No one knows more about feelings than I do, Marsha. If you'd looked properly at your zodiac phone, you will know that I am Selene Luna, also the moon.'

Another from the nut club, I thought. I'd had enough of her, whoever she was. I was dying. I wanted proper sympathy with soft words, kind looks. Presents.

'Look, Selene,' I said, 'I don't know what the game is here with the planet theme or whatever. Is it a monthly thing that some mad doctor dreamed up? Like, let's cheer up the patients by playing dress-up games? Like, last month you were all vegetables, this month you've all decided to be planets. It's fine. It's nice, it's creative and I am sure some of the patients love it. It cheers them up, distracts them from their problems. We did something similar at our school one year and on the second Friday of each month we had to go to school dressed as a character out of history. But what is happening to me is major. I haven't got time to play games. I am very, very ill.'

'No, you're not.'

'Yes, I am.'

'No. You're not.'

'Yes, I am. I heard you saying . . .'

Selene rolled her eyes. 'Typical Aries. Always eavesdropping. Always thinking people are talking about you. It's not always about you, you know. There are other signs of the zodiac.'

'What do you mean? It's not always about me?'

Selene glanced over at Amy. 'We were talking about someone else. Not you.'

I glanced over to Amy's bed where she appeared to be asleep. 'Ohmigod. Amy.'

Selene nodded. 'And we weren't saying that she's going to die either. She's in for a tough time, but the condition she has is one of the few cancers that is manageable. People hear the word cancer, the big C, and think that it automatically means the end. It doesn't. There are so many different types of it, some curable, some manageable, some sadly not. But Amy should come through. It will be a long haul. She has to keep fighting, but the hospital can help her.'

I felt so stupid. Embarrassed. Ashamed. And relieved. All in the same moment. 'So I am not going to die?'

Selene shook her head. 'Yes, you are. I thought we'd established that. Just not any time soon.'

'So what are you doing here asking me about my feelings?' I asked, then lowered my voice. 'Shouldn't you be over there with . . .'

'Marsha. Don't you get it? Didn't Mario tell you? You are Zodiac Girl this month. Girls who are chosen to be Zodiac Girl are picked because either they are at a turning point in their life or because they have something to do. Sometimes both. We, the ten planets, are here to assist. My role is to help you get in touch with your feelings as they will guide you. So, once again, Marsha Leibowitz, how are you feeling?'

My brain felt like it was going to explode. I wasn't going to die. But that lovely gentle girl in the bed across the ward might. I could still go home, continue with my life. She might not be able to.

'How am I feeling? How am I feeling? Confused. More confused than I ever have in my life? In fact . . . I think, I think . . . I may be having a mental breakdown.'

Selene laughed again. She was really beginning to annoy me. Irritation, add that to the pot of feelings, I thought.

'Breakdown? Excellent,' said Selene. 'Break down to break through. You'll get there. I'm sure you will. Aries is a strong sign. And, don't forget, we're here to help.'

With that, she got up to go. I watched her disappear down the ward and out of the double doors. So what am I supposed to do or feel? I asked myself as I glanced back at Amy who appeared to be sleeping peacefully.

Chapter Eleven

Entertainment

After the excitement of the morning, the ward grew quiet and I grew fidgety once again. In my mind, I replayed the conversations that I'd had with Selene and Mario over and over. We're here to help, they'd both said. In that case, I thought, I'll have another look at my phone. I pulled it out and texted in:

Am bored. Zodiac Girl needs entertainment.

Then I pressed SEND. Seconds later, the phone bleeped that I had a message.

Am dispatching the troops. Had to wait until the planets were aligned in a harmonious way! Keep fighting. Mario

Five seconds later, the double door to the ward burst open and in cycled Uri on his unicyle. He was wearing a white doctor's coat and a red nose and he was juggling bed pans! My jaw must have fallen open – the whole effect was hysterical. Ohmigod, I thought as he cycled past, grinning and waving at me a second before catching a flying bed pan.

'Uri,' I called. 'Stop it! You'll get into trouble.' Any minute now, security is going to come rushing in and haul him out, I thought.

'Heard that you were bored,' he said as he cycled backwards down the ward. Skye sat up to watch. Even Amy lifted her head up a little. The nurses came out of their little end room and watched with big smiles on their faces. Why aren't they freaked out? I wondered as Uri got off his cycle and began to juggle mugs from the tea trolley. Four, six, eight in the air. He really was very good at it. After his juggling act, he disappeared to one of the sections I couldn't see. I called Cheryl over.

'What's going on? Why haven't you stopped him?' I asked.

'Why would we? He's Uri. He's a clown doctor. He comes in occasionally to entertain the children's and teenage ward and he doesn't half help cheer people up.'

Bit of a coincidence if you ask me, I thought. Two seconds after I send out a cry for help, he appears. Hmm? In the next section, I could hear oos and ahs and laugher, and it wasn't long before Uri appeared in our section. He made a low bow, which was very funny because he bent over to his knees then to his feet then his head seemed to dip past his toes and along the floor as if he was made of elastic before pulling himself back up. 'For our resident Zodiac Girl and her friends,' he said, and went over to Skye. He got out his stethoscope and put it on the top of her head.

'Hmm,' he said as he pretended to listen to her brain. 'A very serious problem indeed. Oh dear. Oh dear. Oh dear. I think we need to do a transplant. A . . .' He hesitated then produced a red nose similar to the one that he was wearing and put it over Skye's nose. She laughed and Uri pulled a red balloon with something wrapped in a red shiny wrapper on the end of the string from behind her ear. He presented it to her and said, 'Belgian chocolate, the very best.'

Her face lit up. 'My favourite,' she said.

Next he went along to Amy's bed. This time he placed his stethoscope over her ear. She giggled.

'Oh my,' he said. 'What have we here? I think we need to do a CAT scan to find the source of the problem.' From one of his pockets, he produced a black toy cat. 'Now lie back.'

Amy giggled again and did as she was told while Uri waved the cat at arm's length over her, from head to toe. 'Now that is a CAT scan,' he said. 'Not scary at all, is it?'

Amy shook her head and smiled. Uri stuffed the cat back into his pocket and then he began to writhe. It looked as if there were something alive under his coat. A small moving lump, like a little creature. 'Oh. Oh,' cried Uri as he squirmed about. 'Someone wants to come and say hello.' He pulled a white teddy bear out from nowhere. From thin air. It really was magic because the bear seemed to grow before our eyes. Uri placed the bear next to Amy on the pillow, then he leaned over and put his stethoscope on the bear's chest and pretended to listen to its heartbeat.

'Uh-huh. Uh-huh,' he said, and looked at Amy. 'This bear has been very ill and very fed up and away from his mummy and daddy bear. He needs a lot of cuddles and love. Can you give it to him?'

Amy's eyes glistened with tears. She cuddled the bear close to her and nodded.

And then he came to me. 'So. What for the resident Zodiac Girl? Are you missing anything?'

'Um . . . I don't know. Something to do in here?'

'No. No, it's not that. It's . . .' He placed his stethoscope on my arm. 'Ah yes. You need a funny bone.' He reached into his pockets and pulled out a toy dog bone, large and pink with yellow stars on it. He put it in my hand. 'There, that will do the trick. If there are any more problems with the arm, I suggest that you take one of these three times a day.'

I decided to play along with him even though it was all a bit childish. 'And how am I supposed to swallow one of those three times a day?'

'Like this,' said Uri, and he took the bone, which was as big as my hand, stuffed it into his mouth – miraculously, it went in – swallowed and then opened his mouth to show me that it was empty.

'How? Wha—? How did you do that?'

Uri grinned. 'Magic. Now look under your pillow.'

I looked under my pillow and there was the bone. And with it were two miniature bones.

Uri clapped his hands. 'And, look, it's had babies! Baby bones.' He picked up the two small ones and tossed one to Skye and one to Amy, who were watching with big smiles on their faces. 'Here's a spare funny bone for you two in case you ever need one.'

'Thanks,' said Skye.

'Yeah, thanks,' said Amy.

Uri turned back to me and produced a book of crossword puzzles from up his sleeve. 'And these are for you to pass the time,' he said.

I took the book. I hate crossword puzzles. I tried not to look disappointed because all his other tricks had been really good.

'Er . . . thanks.'

'Only joking,' he said, and he produced another packet wrapped in silver wrapping paper from his other sleeve.

I ripped off the paper and gasped. It was a portable

DVD player and some DVDs: *High School Musical,
Enchanted* and *St Trinian's.*

'Wow, awesome,' I said, because *High School Musical* is
one of my all time favourite movies ever. 'Thank you so
much.'

He indicated Amy and Skye. 'Watch with your new
friends. Friends are important wherever you are,' he
said, and then he robot danced backwards along the
ward. His dancing was very comical and by this time,
everyone in my section had big grins on their faces,
including the tea lady.

'Awesome,' I said out loud as Uri did a comical fall then
got up and staggered out through the ward doors.

'Yeah,' said Skye. 'He's cool.'

When the atmosphere settled down again, I began to
wonder. Was it a coincidence that he'd turned up
seconds after my request? Maybe it wasn't. But Cheryl
had said that he came by occasionally so perhaps it just
happened to coincide with my text message and was
nothing to do with a request on my zodiac phone. Well,
there's only one way to find out if there's any
connection. I have to try my zodiac mobile again.

I found the text option and typed in:

Am starving for some decent food. Please send
scrumptious supplies.

I pressed SEND and off the message went.

Nothing happened. I kept looking hopefully at the double doors but the only people who came through were a doctor, a nurse and a cleaner. I felt my spirits sink again. So Uri's clown-doctor visit had been a coincidence after all. I shifted about and tried to get comfortable. Amy looked like she was asleep and Skye was listening to her iPod so I started to watch a DVD. After about ten minutes, the doors opened. A big jolly man bustled in with what looked like a basket of goodies on his left arm.

'Hey, Joe,' called Cheryl.

'Hey there, Nursie,' he said, and began to dole out little packages in brown paper wrappings. When he got to our section, he gave me a wink.

'I believe you called,' he said.

'I . . . I er . . .'

'Mario is your guardian, yes?' said the man.

'Um, yeah, sort of, er . . . I'm new to all this . . .' I began.

'Zodiac Girl?' he asked.

I nodded and the man came and leant over me so that the others couldn't hear him. 'I'm Jupiter, but people call me Joe,' he whispered. 'Best not to let on about the planet connection or else people might think you're mad. Just know that Mario is on your case and we're all here for you and will do what we can.'

'Oh. OK, thank you,' I said. 'And, yes, I sort of know

about the planet thing. Theme of the month, yeah?'

'Theme? No. But never mind. Mario's the one who has to explain it all.'

'He did say something about the planets being here in human form but . . . you can't have come from a planet. That's impossible, isn't it?'

'Why?' said Joe. 'Do you know where you came from?'

'A village down the road.'

'I mean before that. Before you were here as Marsha?'

'Before I was born?'

Joe nodded.

'Um, no, course not. No one does.'

'Well, maybe you were from a star,' said Joe. 'A star up in the sky.'

'Like an alien?'

'No – like energy. But enough of this kind of talk. I'm not here to give a lecture about where we've come from. Just know that there are many things we don't understand, Marsha – many things defy logic – don't close your mind to anything or say something isn't possible. Now, I understand that you don't approve of the hospital food so far, yes?'

'Yes.'

'So what do you fancy?'

'I love hot chocolate. And I love blueberry muffins. They're my favourite. Dad always gets them for me when I'm not well.'

Joe beamed. 'Well, isn't that a coincidence, because I just happen to have . . .' He produced a muffin and a paper mug filled with a steaming liquid. He handed both to me and tapped the side of his nose as if to say that we had a secret between us.

As he went off down the ward distributing his goodies, I sipped my drink. It was the best hot chocolate I had ever tasted. Thick and creamy with just the right amount of sweetness. And the muffin was melt-in-your-mouth fabulous.

After he'd done his rounds, I called Cheryl over.

'So where did he come from?' I asked.

'Osbury,' she said. 'He has a deli there. He pops in when he can with a few extras for the patients. There's a whole family of them living and working there and they come in as volunteers for the hospital from time to time. I wish they could come in more, in fact . . .'

After Joe, Cheryl announced that someone was coming in from a local beauty salon to do pampering treatments. Half an hour later a lady called Nessa arrived with two assistants. I couldn't help but stare at her. She looked like a model, no, even more beautiful than that. She looked like a goddess – tall, with blonde hair and a perfect oval face with blue eyes.

'So oo's for being pampered,' she said with a broad Essex accent.

Amy, Skye and I all held up a hand and the two

assistants went to their beds and Nessa came over to mine.

'Awright, doll?' she asked.

I nodded. 'Yes. Actually I'm having an OK day.'

She smiled, sat at the end of the bed and peeled back the covers and began to give me a foot massage. It was pure heaven. While she was doing it, I looked at the names on my phone. Nessa, Venus, it said.

'Are you part of the special club?' I asked.

'What do you mean, love?' asked Nessa. I showed my phone. 'I won this on the Internet and it has ten names on it. Something to do with astrology and planets.'

'That's right, duck,' said Nessa. 'You're this month's Zodiac Girl, right? Ya met yer guardian?'

'Mario, yes, otherwise known as Mars. And um . . . according to my phone, Nessa . . . you're Venus?'

'That's right. Planet of love and beauty. I run a beauty shop in Osbury.'

'And you work as a volunteer in the hospital?'

'Sometimes. We all signed up for a bit, ready for when ya were comin' in.'

'For me?'

'Yeah, cos ya're Zodiac Girl and we're 'ere to 'elp. Like imagine if we told the nursin' staff that we were the planets 'ere in human form. They'd think we were a bunch of nutters and never let us in. We have to think up ways to get around. Ways to be accepted in normal society. It was in yer chart that somethin' like this would happen to ya, and ya might end up in here for a bit, so Mario told us to get ready. To start here as volunteers.'

'I can see your point,' I said. 'Yes, they might think that you were all mad.' Because you are! I thought. Either that or my anaesthetic hasn't worn off and I am having a strange dream.

Whatever the reason, I don't mind, I thought after she'd gone and I'd looked at the phone to see that three hours had gone by since they had arrived. Are they volunteers with overactive imaginations who are a little bonkers? Or not? I wondered. If not, it's like having the modern-day equivalent of an Aladdin's lamp. I felt a rush of excitement flood through me as I considered what else the zodiac phone might be able to do.

Chapter Twelve

My Bee-ootiful Sisters

'Why are you crying? And what the heck happened to your hair?' asked Cissie that evening when she arrived with Mum and Eleanor, and I burst into tears at the sight of them. The three of them looked so lovely and familiar when they walked in that I couldn't help it. Skye glanced up at them. People always stared at my sisters because they were so striking and they looked particularly so in the brightly lit ward. Cissie had obviously just come from ballet class and was dressed in fuchsia leggings and a pink T-shirt. Eleanor was wearing a tiny denim skirt over thick black tights. She had the longest legs and knew how to show them off.

'I'm just so pleased to see you,' I replied. 'I . . . I thought I'd never see you again.'

Eleanor sat on a chair to the right of my bed. 'Why not? You're such a drama queen, Marsha. You've only hurt your wrist. Now, when I was in hospital, it really was serious. Remember, Mum, when I fell off my horse. The doctors thought I'd never walk again.'

'Yes——' Mum began.

'Rubbish,' said Cissie as she sat on a chair to the left of my bed. 'It was a sprain, nothing more, but, when I was in hospital after my fall, the doctors thought I might have damaged my brain——'

'You did. No doubt about it,' said Eleanor, and she pulled a face at Cissie.

Mum settled herself on the end of the bed. 'Now, girls,' she began.

'As I was saying,' Cissie interrupted in a raised voice. 'I had concussion. Now that is serious.'

'Nonsense,' said Eleanor. 'They didn't even keep you in overnight.'

Normally, I would have joined in with gusto. It was always like this with my sisters, each of us competing to outdo the other, whatever was at stake. Our voices would get louder and louder in the fight to be heard. But today it felt like my birthday, like Christmas, like the most special special day because I'd had a lovely morning and I wasn't going to die. Least not yet. I sat there beaming at my gorgeous sisters and my beautiful mother.

'What's the matter, Marsha?' asked Cissie. 'You're looking at us strangely.'

'Yeah. Are you on drugs?' asked Eleanor.

'No. Just really, really pleased to see you. I had forgotten how beautiful you all are.'

'She's definitely on drugs,' said Cissie.

'You know guys, I really love you,' I said.

'Whoa! Maybe you did damage more than your wrist,' said Eleanor. 'Mum, she's gone mental.'

Mum smiled at me. 'Not at all. I think that's sweet, Marsha, and we love you too.'

'No, we don't,' chorused Cissie and Eleanor, but they looked slightly dewy eyed when they said it.

'So what did happen to the hair?' asked Eleanor.

I put my hand up to my head. I was longing for a hairwash. 'It was for a part in the school show. Ice Queen,' I replied.

Mum patted my hand. 'Marsha got the part, didn't you, dear? But er . . . she can't do it now.'

I suddenly realized that I didn't mind about not playing the Ice Queen any more. I was going to live. I was going to get out of hospital. There would be other parts. Other shows. 'It's OK,' I said. 'There are more important things.'

'That's the attitude,' said Mum, but she looked surprised.

'So, kid, when are you getting out of here?' asked Cissie.

I was in such a good mood I didn't even mind that she'd called me kid. Usually that would have started a full-blown argument because she knows I hate it. 'Tomorrow, if everything's OK. In fact, Mum, they fixed the X-ray machine and I had mine redone just before you came in. When Dr Sam's had a chance to look them over, which the nurses think will be in the morning, I'm out of here.'

'Cool,' said Cissie, and she split the goodies that Mum had brought in and proceeded to help herself to the chocolates. 'No point in letting these go to waste, then.'

Eleanor opened one of the magazines and began to read. 'And you'll be able to read these at home so I may as well have a look now as I'm busy the rest of the week.'

I didn't even mind that. 'Help yourself,' I said. 'Help yourself.'

On the other side of the ward I saw Amy glance over and smile. I smiled back at her.

As soon as the visitors had gone for the evening, I got out of my bed and went over to Amy's. Her arm was attached to some kind of drip. She was awake and saw me looking at it. 'Blood transfusion,' she said. 'Sometimes they give me one before they start my chemotherapy. You'll see me change colour as it goes through. I go from pale to pink.'

'How long are you in for?' I asked.

'Only three days this time. I come in once every three weeks for a couple of days and they do my treatment. I'm on round four. Two more to go.'

'Then what?'

Amy shrugged. 'Don't know exactly. More treatment.'

I looked at the blood sack. 'Does that make you feel weird?'

Amy shook her head. 'Nah. Makes me feel better. It's the chemo that makes me feel weird. After it, I have one week of feeling awful, one week of feeling medium awful and one week of feeling almost all right and then I have to come back and start the process all over again.'

'It must be terrible. You poor thing.'

Amy shrugged and glanced away.

'God. Sorry. Me and my big mouth. Just say if you don't want to talk about it.'

'I don't want to, if you don't mind. It's . . . it's boring. I'd like to hear about you, though. Tell me all about you and why you're in here.'

'No probs,' I said with a grin. 'Permission . . . no, an invite to talk about myself. You don't know what you've let yourself in for.' For the next ten minutes, I filled her in on all the events of the last few days apart from the eavesdropping bit.

'I bet you'd have made a great Ice Queen,' she said.

'Yeah. But guess not many Ice Queens have a thumping great plaster cast on their arm.'

Amy laughed and then looked at me kindly. 'You looked a bit upset before. Have you . . . have you . . . had some bad news that you haven't told me about?'

'Uh . . .' For a moment I felt lost for words. How could I tell her that I had been upset, but only because I thought what was happening to her was happening to me? And what a relief it had been when I'd found out it wasn't me after all. I so wished I could give her some news. Like that I was a good fairy and could wave a magic wand to make whatever was wrong with her go away. 'No biggie. It's just so boring in here. Like the hours seem to stretch out until forever.'

Amy rolled her eyes. 'Tell me about it. Some hospitals have recreation rooms where there are things to do, but not this one. It wasn't in the budget, apparently.'

'Oh, yeah. I remember now. A girl at our school was trying to organize a charity event to raise money for a recreation wing. She was looking for people to perform.' Now that I'd met Amy and experienced for myself how endless days in hospital could be, I felt ashamed of the way I had turned Sophie down. I decided I'd better change the subject before Amy asked if I was going to be in Sophie's concert and realized what a selfish cow I was. 'But come on – fair's fair. I've told about me. What about you?'

'Not a lot to tell. I'm thirteen. One sister who lives in Australia. Music is my thing. I like all sorts. Um. Got ill about six months ago. Boring boring, don't want to talk about it. Wish it hadn't happened. Felt it wasn't fair. There are so many things I still want to do and having to come back here again and again really gets in the way. I moaned and groaned a lot, but now I think what's the point? I try to get on with it, make the best I can of it. Get in here, get out as fast as poss. Know what I mean?'

'Oh, yeah. But you'll be out soon.'

'For a while. It's part of my life now and I just have to accept that. I try not to feel sorry for myself, though of course some days I do.'

'Well, I think you're amazing. If it was me, I'd be a total mess.'

Amy smiled. 'No you wouldn't. You deal with it day by day.'

At that moment, the nurse came over to change Amy's drip and she shooed me away.

'Laters,' I said. 'Want to watch a DVD when they've finished with you?'

Amy beamed back at me. 'Yeah. What you got?'

'*High School Musical* and *St Trinian's*.'

Amy gave me a thumbs up as the nurse swished the curtains round her.

On the way back to my bed, I looked over to see Skye. I thought I might ask her to join us, but she had her iPod headphones in and her eyes closed, so I decided best not to disturb her. As I climbed back on my own bed, I felt so thankful that this really would be the last night and soon I'd be free.

Chapter Thirteen

Going Home

Stepping out from the hospital reception area the next morning into the light of the car park felt like emerging from a bad dream. All the colours in the outside world seemed more vivid, all the sounds louder.

I spotted Mum's car immediately. Silly thing – she'd tied a bunch of pink balloons on the back. I gave her a hug to show her that I appreciated the gesture.

Mum supported my arm while I hobbled over to the car and got into the passenger seat. As she started up the car and drove through the traffic, I gazed out of the window. It felt so good to actually be going home, to be back in the world where things were happening.

The drive to our house took about twenty minutes and when Mum opened our front door I felt like I was being let into paradise. Everything was how I remembered but somehow brighter and more comfortable-looking. I inhaled the familiar smell of charred toast and strawberry – from the scented candles that Cissie always burned in her room. Lovely. We went through to the kitchen and there on the table was a chocolate cake with shiny glistening icing.

'Cissie and Eleanor stayed up and baked it for you last night after they got back from the hospital,' said Mum. 'Chocolate fudge, your favourite.'

She cut us both a slice and we sat at the kitchen table to eat them with tall glasses of milk. I looked over at Mum and smiled at her. 'This is the happiest day of my whole life,' I said.

Mum laughed. 'Let's see how long that feeling lasts,' she said.

'Oh it will, it will,' I said. 'I will never take anything here for granted ever again.'

Mum raised an eyebrow as if to say she still didn't believe me.

After the cake, I wandered upstairs and poked my head in all the rooms as if I were going around the house for the first time. Our lovely white bathroom that smelt of jasmine soap instead of antiseptic, like the shampoo that Nurse Abbie had used to wash my hair at hospital this morning. How could I have ever thought our house was too small? It was perfect. Next was Cissie's room with the cornflower-blue walls and all her posters of famous ballet dancers. Further along the corridor was Eleanor's room, painted baby pink but now covered in so many posters of boy bands you could hardly see the walls. It was chaos as usual in there with drawers and cupboards open – their contents spilling out, pots of nail varnish and make-up strewn on her dressing table.

'Lovely, lovely,' I said. Both rooms looked so homely. At the back next to my room was Mum and Dad's. I opened the door. It felt so peaceful in there. A white bedspread and curtains and lavender walls with a neat pile of books on both their sides of the bed. History books on Dad's side, gardening, recipe books and magazines on Mum's.

And, at last, my own room looking out over the back garden.

'Hello, room,' I said as I opened the door. I went and sat for a moment on the window seat, looking out over the lawn covered in orange and gold leaves fallen from the trees. Then I got up and sat on my bed, sighing at how comfy it felt. I lay back. 'Ahhhhh, lovely jubbly bed. I love you. I've missed you,' I said, sinking back. I fell into a light sleep only to be woken by the sound of the doorbell. A few minutes later, Lois appeared at my door. She bounded over and was about to give me a huge hug when she remembered my arm.

'Whoops,' she said. 'How is it? How does it feel?'

'Better,' I said. 'It's OK but I feel fanlubblytastic.'

'Why? What's happened? Has anything happened with the zodiac people?'

I filled her in on all their comings and goings in the

hospital and her eyes grew large with amazement. 'Awesome,' she said.

'Yeah. Apparently Mario, my guardian, got them all to be volunteers especially for me.'

'You're so lucky,' said Lois. 'So now what?'

I shrugged.

At that exact moment, the zodiac phone rang in my pocket. I pulled it out. It was Mario.

'Zodiac Girl,' he said.

'Mario,' I replied in exactly the same sombre tone and gave Lois a thumbs up. She grinned back at me.

'You're out?'

'I'm out.'

'You know what you have to do now?'

'Yes. Have a great big bubble bath. Mum's cooking my fave lunch, then a bit of telly.'

'No. That's not it at all.'

'Why not? I just got home.'

'I know. But what are you going to do next?'

'I don't know. Er . . . get better. Go back to school?'

'Marsha,' said Mario in an exasperated tone of voice. 'Can't you get it through your thick skull? You are Aries. Aries are the movers and shakers of the zodiac.'

'That's me. So?'

'They are the leaders. The ones that make things happen. What are you going to make happen?'

Lois was making faces at me. 'What's he saying?'

I shrugged my shoulders and made a face as if to say, I don't know.

'Mario, can't you just tell me if I am supposed to do something?'

'No, I can't. It has to come from you and I would have thought it was obvious by now.'

'Give us a clue,' I said cheekily.

'Clue! CLUE!' he roared. 'That's all you've had since your time started. I don't know. I really don't. Haven't you learned anything?'

'Yeah. That I don't like being in hospital. That's what I learned.'

I could hear Mario sigh in a weary way at the other end of the phone. 'Look,' he said. 'Sleep on it, why don't you?'

'Sounds as good a plan as any,' I said, and he sighed again then clicked off.

'What?' asked Lois.

'I don't know. He says I am supposed to do something. That I am a leader.' I caught a glimpse of my reflection. I still looked weird with my white brittle hair. 'Maybe that I shouldn't have dyed my hair? Maybe I should get a new style?'

Lois giggled and nodded.

Chapter Fourteen

Back to Business

Thump, thump, thump. Someone was banging on the bathroom door. 'Marsha! Get a move on. What are you doing in there? Taking a nap?' Cissie called.

Another thump then Eleanor's voice. 'Yeah. There's a queue out here. You're not the only one who has to get washed and out this morning.'

'Give me a break,' I said, opening the door. 'It's not easy with only one arm, you know, and a sore ankle.'

'Not easy with ownwee one arm,' my horrible sisters chorused together, while pulling silly faces at me.

'You two have no idea what it is like to live in pain,' I said as I pushed past them. They didn't. Even the simplest of tasks, like getting dressed, is hard with only one working arm. Luckily my ankle was feeling a lot better – almost back to normal – but I wasn't going to tell them that.

They both creased up laughing. Cissie held the back of her palm up to her forehead. 'You haf no idea vot it is like to lif in pain,' she said in a stupid fake Russian accent. 'My life is so trageek.' Eleanor took advantage of Cissie being distracted to get into the bathroom and shut the door behind her.

'Oi! I was next,' cried Cissie as soon as she realized, and then the thumping on the door began again.

'Be quiet out there,' Dad called from the bedroom.

Indie music was blasting in Eleanor's bedroom, world music from Cissie's and I could hear the radio on down below in the kitchen.

'This house is SO noisy!' I said, heading back into my bedroom. 'And TOO small.'

It wasn't even a week since I had left the hospital and it was back to business as usual. My sisters' sympathy had lasted about twenty-four hours, about as long as the chocolate fudge cake which they had baked for me and which they polished off when they got home from school. It had been good being back to classes for the first few days – I had been the centre of attention and everyone had wanted to sign my cast. But they soon lost interest and moved on to other things like the school show. The hurt that I couldn't play the Ice Queen had soon come back when I saw that Carol Kennedy was playing my part.

I'd tried to talk Mrs Pierson into letting me do the part with my injured arm and ankle. I said it would show what a liberal school we were – letting the less than fortunate take main parts. She smiled, patted me on the head and called me a poppet, which made me CROSS.

I'd bumped into Mario a few times along the corridor near the gym and each time he asked the same thing: 'Got it yet, Zodiac Girl?'

Each time, I gave him the same reply. 'Nope.'

I wasn't being difficult. I really didn't know what he was on about.

'Marsha, are you ready?' Mum called up the stairs. Her sympathy hadn't lasted long either – once she knew that I wasn't going to die, she had soon reverted to being her usual bossy self.

So much for being a Zodiac Girl, I thought as I struggled into my jacket. All the treats and fun of that had dried up as soon as I'd got home apart from one text message saying that Mercury was retrograde so it would be a quiet time for a week or so.

'Almost,' I called back. It was time for my first physio session at the hospital.

The physiotherapy wing was in a separate part of the hospital to where I had stayed previously. It was a modern building with plenty of light streaming in through tall windows.

'This is nice, isn't it?' said Mum as we made our way to the waiting room. 'Not as depressing as that other place.'

'I just hope it doesn't hurt,' I said, hobbling along.

Mum hugged me. 'It will help,' she said.

There was only one other person in the waiting room when we got there. Skye. Despite her being so cool with me when we were in the hospital ward, I felt pleased to see her. We had shared an experience that no one else – especially my sisters – could understand. She glanced over and jutted her chin out. I suppose that was her way of saying hi.

'Hey,' I said. 'You're out.'

She nodded. 'Time off for good behaviour.'

Mum went off to find a Ladies so I sat next to Skye.

'How's it been?' I asked.

She shrugged. 'Better than being in here,' she said.

'Ditto. My own pillows. My own bed.'

'Been up to see Amy?' she asked.

I shook my head. I hadn't even thought about Amy in the last few weeks. I felt ashamed. 'No. I er . . . I thought she went home in between her treatments.'

'Not this time,' said Skye. 'Something to do with her blood count being low and her immune system being weak, so they want to keep an eye on her.'

'Poor thing,' I said. 'I'll go up after the physio.'

Skye nodded, then got out her iPod and put the headphones in her ears. I got the message. Conversation over. I found my magazine and started to read. After sitting reading for half an hour, a nurse called Skye's name and mine.

Skye hobbled up. I stayed where I was.

'Must be a mistake,' I said. 'I'll wait here.'

Skye nodded then shuffled off down the corridor and disappeared into a side room. Moments later, the nurse called again. 'Marsha Leibowitz.'

'You'd better go, love,' said Mum.

I got up and made my way along the corridor and into the room where Dr Sam was sitting and Skye was standing over by the window.

'Hey, Marsha. How's the arm and the ankle?' he asked.

'Good. Both a bit stiff.'

'Then this will be timely. Now I bet you're wondering why I've got you both in here together.'

I nodded and Skye glared at him.

'Well, Marsha, there's not a lot we can do for your wrist at this stage, so today will be to keep your ankle improving. Your physiotherapy is going to be really similar to Skye's and it's always more fun to do it with a pal, so I thought I'd put you both in together.'

Skye and I exchanged unenthusiastic glances. If she were going to continue being unfriendly, then so was I.

Dr Sam left the room and a lady in a white coat came in and introduced herself as Martha. She asked us to stand up then put us through a series of exercises. It felt good to me to do the rotations and stretches, but I could see that Skye was finding it more difficult. I glanced at her at one point and her face looked strained and pale.

'Take it easy, Skye,' said Martha.

Skye grimaced. 'Yeah, don't try to run before I can walk,' she said.

'Something like that,' said Martha.

Mum was waiting for me when we got out.

'Ready to go?' she asked.

I shook my head. 'Can you give me a few minutes? I want to go up to see someone on the ward.'

'Sure,' said Mum. 'I'll go and grab a coffee from the café.'

We made our way over to the main hospital building and Mum left me at the lift. I didn't have to wait long, and was soon back on the ward. It felt strange being there again and I felt a strong sense of relief that I wasn't going to have to stay this time.

Nurse Cheryl came out of her office. 'Hey, if it isn't our little marshmallow. How're you doing, Marsha?'

'Great,' I said. 'Least, OK. I came to see Amy. Is she still here?'

Nurse Cheryl nodded and looked over to the section I'd been in. 'She's been missing you girls, I think.'

I crossed over to the section where I'd stayed and saw that there was only one bed that was occupied and that was Amy's. She appeared to be asleep and I was about to leave when she opened her eyes and her face lit up.

'Marsha,' she said. 'I'd been hoping that you might come back. Skye was in earlier.' She sat up and patted the end of the bed. 'How are you?'

I glanced over at the empty beds. 'I'm doing fine, thanks, but . . . is there no one else in here with you?'

She shook her head. 'No. The nurses say it's lovely and quiet now, but . . .' Her eyes filled with tears. 'It's been awful, especially at night. I know we didn't talk much when you were in and Skye kept herself to herself most of the time, but at least you were there. I knew there was someone in the other beds and I didn't feel so alone.'

I reached out and took her hand. I felt like my heart was going to break. I was free, but she was still in here, away from her family and home. 'What about during the day? Has the clown doctor been in?'

Amy shook her head. 'I asked about him, but apparently there's only him and he goes around a few hospitals, not just this one. One of the nurses told me that they didn't have the budget for entertainment.' She smiled. 'He was great, though, wasn't he? He really took my mind of things for a while.'

I nodded then I had an idea. I got up and did the funny dancing that I used to do when I was younger to entertain aunties at Christmas. It's a bit of moonwalking then robot dancing. As I was dancing, I didn't notice that Skye had come in and was standing behind me. I noticed Amy looking over my shoulder, so I turned.

Skye gave me one of her chin-jut nods. I jutted my chin back at her.

'Not bad, newbie,' she said. 'Don't let me stop you.' She started counting time by snapping her fingers, so I started dancing again. Slowly, Skye came over and began to move in time with me, mainly her upper body but she could move her feet a little with the help of her crutch. Despite her injured ankle, I could see that she had natural rhythm and could dance, if a little slowly because of her foot. It was as if we tuned into each other and went into this spontaneous routine.

When we'd finished, Amy clapped. 'Brilliant,' she said. 'Hip hop heroines.'

'Yeah, cool,' said Skye.

I grinned back at her. 'Thanks.' I turned back to Amy. 'Hey, I have to go now. My mum is waiting downstairs, but I will come back and visit.'

'Promise?'

'Promise,' I said.

'And I can stay a while longer,' said Skye. 'My mum's not picking me up for another fifteen minutes.'

'Great,' said Amy.

'Laters,' said Skye, and, for the first time, she smiled at me.

'Laters,' I said.

That night, before I went to sleep, I checked my

zodiac phone and there was a message from Mario saying:

Time is running out, have you got it yet?

I got into bed and lay staring at the ceiling. Got what? Got what? I asked myself. I couldn't concentrate for long, though. I couldn't stop thinking about Amy. I was home, comfy and in familiar surroundings. She was still in hospital and although the staff were lovely and did what they could I knew that it felt strange at night with the distant noises down the corridors and comings and goings on the ward. And then it was as if a light bulb flashed on in my head. That was it! That was what Mario had been waiting for. I climbed out of bed, got my zodiac phone and replied to his message.

Got it. I know exactly what I have to do!

Chapter Fifteen

It's Showtime, Folks

'You want to do what?' asked Dad as the family sat around having breakfast on Saturday morning.

'I need to raise about . . . um, a million pounds ought to do it,' I said.

Dad almost spat his coffee out. Mum, Cissie and Eleanor burst out laughing.

'Full points for having a goal,' said Mum.

'Yeah. But . . . how exactly are you going to get this million pounds?' Cissie asked.

'OK, maybe not a million, then, maybe just about five hundred grand. I haven't actually researched my figures yet.'

All assembled fell about laughing again like I was telling the best jokes ever. 'Not researched my figures yet,' Cissie mimicked in a fake posh voice.

Dad was the first to make an attempt to straighten his face. 'Sorry, Marsha. We shouldn't be laughing. Now explain what all this is about.'

'You can laugh. You'll see. I'm an Aries and we're the

leaders of the zodiac, in case you didn't know. The movers and the shakers. We make things happen,' I said.

'So what are you going to make happen?' asked Eleanor.

'I am going to raise enough money to build a recreation wing at the local hospital so that children and teenagers in there can go and chill out or play on computers or listen to music or paint or whatever they feel like. I also need to fund a regular bunch of entertainers to go in for those who can't get out of bed.'

Hah! That shut them up.

'Wow! Good for you,' said Mum, 'but don't you think that's maybe a bit ambitious?'

I shook my head and quoted back our headmaster's favourite quote: 'We have to reach for the stars.'

Cissie giggled and grabbed her bag, which was on the dresser behind us. She pulled out her purse and handed me a coin. 'There's twenty pence, kid,' she said, and she and Eleanor started laughing again.

I got up to leave. 'I should have known better than to expect you lowlifes to take me seriously.'

'We do, sweetheart,' said Mum, 'but you have to think this through a bit.'

'I know that,' I said. 'I'm not stupid. I am going to work out a business plan.'

Dad was doing his best to keep his face straight, but he

couldn't do it. I gave him a filthy look.

'No, no,' he spluttered. 'I think it's marvellous. You make me very proud.'

'I am going to change the world. You'll see,' I said, and I left the room, slamming the door behind me so that there was no doubt about how I felt.

Lois was more understanding.

'Great. So how are you going to do that?' she asked after I'd told her my plan over the phone. I looked down at the blank page in my note pad in front of me. 'Er . . . Well . . . You got any ideas?'

'Um . . . No.'

'OK. No problem. Let's go to the library. There must be a book on how to make millions. Meet you there in half an hour.'

Our local library was only round the corner from where we lived and I got there before Lois. I decided to call Mario while I stood outside waiting. He sounded pleased to hear from me.

'Hi, Zodiac Girl. I got your message. So you know what to do?'

'Yep. Raise money for a recreation wing at the hospital.'

I heard a sharp intake of breath, then he chuckled. 'OK. Good. How much are you aiming for?'

'About a million.'

I heard another sharp intake of breath. 'Good. Good to be ambitious.'

'Is that what you were waiting to hear?' I asked.

'Sort of. It's always up to the individual Zodiac Girl to decide what she's going to do with her month. Some do a lot, some do very little. With you being Aries, I knew it would be something extraordinary, but, as I said, it had to come from you, so, no, it wasn't exactly what I was waiting to hear.'

'So how do I do it?'

'Ah. Now that has to come from you too.'

'Aren't I supposed to have won a prize or something? And part of that is your help?'

'Right. But you're an Aries. You have to lead.'

I was beginning to get impatient. 'You're not being very helpful.'

'I will be when you tell me what to do.'

'OK, which of your team has anything to do with finance?'

'That would be either Jupiter, which is the planet of expansion so, if it's favourably aspected in your chart, it can mean winnings of some sort as everything it touches expands. And then Pluto is sometimes known as the Lord of Wealth so get those two together in a chart and it could be good depending on where they are.'

'Can you look at my chart and see where they are?'

'Can do. I'll get back to you. Wait until you've heard from me, though, won't you?'

I could see Lois coming down the pavement and I waved. 'OK. Maintain radio contact, Mario. We're not through yet.'

'Glad to hear it,' he said, and clicked off.

Lois linked her arm through my good one and we went into the library and up to the desk where a tall, thin lady with a wrinkly neck was busy stamping books.

'Excuse me,' I said. 'Where are the reference books?'

'What kind?' she asked without looking up.

'The ones on how to make a lot of money.'

She looked up then with an amused glint in her eye. 'You need to be more specific,' she said. 'You mean like what career can make you money?'

'No. Now. I need to raise about a million, soon, maybe five hundred grand.'

'Don't we all, dear,' she said, and jerked her chin towards a small room off the main part of the library. She looked as if she were having a hard time not laughing. 'You might find something in there. Let me know if you find anything good.' And she went back to her stamping.

I rolled my eyes. 'What is wrong with people that they all find this so funny?'

Lois shrugged. 'Yeah. They don't know you, do they?'

'Do you think I could do it?'

'I think when you set your mind on something you go for it,' she replied.

I pointed up at the sky and did a small kung fu leap into the air. 'Hazah! Zodiac Girl, watch out, she's coming.'

'Shhh,' shushed an old man, who was sitting and reading a newspaper.

'Sorry,' I whispered back. Lois and I tiptoed into the reference library and began to search the shelves.

After half an hour of hauling books down and flicking through, looking for any kind of clue on how to make money fast, I turned to Lois.

'Anything?'

She glanced up from the heavy book she had in front of her and shook her head. 'Corporate this, corporate that and a load of graphs I don't understand, but no make-money-quick schemes. How did you get on?'

'Nothing. I don't think we are going to find the answer here. Let's go and get a juice down the road and rethink the plan.'

Lois saluted. 'Aye, aye, captain.'

We made our way out of the library and along the high street. It was a grey day outside, so we hurried along, eager to get out of the cold. Just before we turned into the doorway at the Juicy Juice bar, a poster in the window caught my eye. Lucky Lotto scratch cards. That was the answer. Spend five pounds and the prize was one million pounds. And Mario had said something about Jupiter, hadn't he? Something about everything it touched meaning expansion. Well, you couldn't get a better expansion than five pounds into a million. I just knew I was going to win.

'How much money have you got on you, Lois?'

Lois put her hand in her pocket. 'Four pounds fifty.'

'And I've got five pounds fifty.' I pointed at the poster for the cards.

'Oh no, we mustn't,' she said. 'My mum said never to waste money on those.'

'Someone's got to win,' I said. 'And I can feel it's going to be me, I mean us. I can feel it in my bones. It's just the amount we need. We could get two. Two goes, double our luck.'

Lois looked unenthusiastic. 'But we wouldn't be able to get a drink then and I'm thirsty.'

'Sacrifices have to be made in the line of honour,' I said. I didn't quite know what I meant, but it sounded good.

'And now you're making me feel guilty,' moaned Lois.

'Don't be such a moaning Minnie,' I said. 'Guilt is good. It means you have a conscience and are really a good person. Now hand over your money.'

Lois gave me her coins but she didn't look happy about it.

'Oh, come on, Lois, cheer up. In this life, there are

winners and losers, and we, my dear, are winners.'

'If you say so,' said Lois, and with a look of regret back at the juice bar, she turned and trudged after me into the newsagent.

I marched up to the counter behind which was a young Indian man who was busy watching a football match on the TV screen on the right of his till.

'Two five-pound scratch cards,' I said in my best confident voice.

It seemed like a particularly exciting moment was happening on the screen and the man barely glanced at me. He peeled off two cards, all the while keeping his attention on the game. 'OH!' he cried as one of the footballers kicked a near miss.

I handed him the money, which he put into his till as if he were on automatic pilot. We were about to leave the shop when he called after me: 'Oi. How old are you?'

'Sixteen,' I said in a deep voice. 'But the cards are not for me, anyhow. They're for my sister for her twenty-first. I thought they'd make an unusual gift.'

The shopkeeper was hardly listening as the players kicked the ball back down to one side of the pitch. As I opened the door to leave, I heard him cry at the TV, 'Go, go GOOOOOO.'

I shut the door behind us and grinned at Lois. 'Well, that was easy! I thought for a minute he wasn't going to sell us the cards.'

'But you told a lie. Your sisters are sixteen and eighteen.'

'White lie,' I said. 'There's a difference and it's for a good cause.'

Lois pointed at a bus shelter over by the church on the green. 'Let's go over there.'

We made our way over to the bench and sat down, ready to scratch our cards.

'I feel so excited,' I said. 'Don't you?'

'A bit,' said Lois. 'Give me one, then, seeing as I paid for it.'

I handed her a card and looked down at mine. 'OK. Ready, steady . . . go.'

And we started scratching. There were four games on the card. On the first, you had to match the winning symbol. I scratched off the winning symbol. It was the letter K. I scratched off the rest. Four letters appeared. N, P, R and X. No K.

'Bummer,' I said. 'How did you do?'

Lois shook her head. 'No match.'

'Well, we have three left,' I said, and began to scratch the rest of the card. In the next game if the amount in the left-hand column under the title YOURS was higher than the amount in the middle column under THEIRS, you won the prize in the third column. We got busy scratching.

YOURS	THEIRS	PRIZE
14	18	£20
23	30	£100,000
34	45	£500
38	39	£1,000,000

'Oh!' I cried as I scratched off the last amounts. 'I almost won. Thirty-eight, thirty-nine, a million!'

'Almost doesn't make it,' said Lois. 'I haven't won either.'

We got busy on the third game. Match three amounts to win. I scratched off £40, £400, £50, £400. 'Oo, oo, I just need one more four hundred,' I said as I continued scratching. But no luck, the other amounts were £4 and £25.

'One last game,' I said. 'This has to be it. Come on, Jupiter, my man. Work your magic.'

The last game was like a fruit machine in that you had to get a row of three the same. I scratched away. Two cherries and a lemon. Two apples and an orange. Two oranges and a cherry. A peach and two lemons. I checked and checked all the games. I could not believe it. I hadn't won a thing.

'Ohmigod, ohmigod,' said Lois as she got to her last row. 'Cherry, cherry, ohmigod, cherry! Marsha, I've won. I've WON!'

I felt a blast of adrenalin flood through me. 'How

much? How much? Scrape off the prize.'

Lois quickly scraped off the last box and her face fell. 'A . . . a pound! Oh no. Is that all?'

'Give it here. That can't be right,' I said, and checked her card for mistakes, but there it was: a pound.

'Well, at least I can go and claim it and we can maybe get a can of something to drink.'

'OK,' I said. 'Or . . . or maybe you could buy one of those pound scratch cards. Maybe we could still win.'

Lois gave me a withering look. 'Marsha, leave it. You stay here while I go to claim our winnings.' She set off for the shop and while I sat waiting my zodiac phone bleeped.

'Hello?' I said.

'Marsha?'

'Yeah.'

'Mario. Today there's a good link to Saturn but there are no good aspects from Jupiter. In fact, it's at a bit of a difficult angle.'

'Too late.'

'What do you mean?'

'I've just gambled and lost.'

'But I told you not to do anything until you heard from me.'

'I . . . I've got to go. My friend's coming back.'

Lois didn't look at all happy. 'The man in the shop wouldn't even give me our pound. He said you'd said you

139

were going to give the cards to your sister and you lied. He said never to go in there ever again or he'll call the police.'

'So not even a drink?'

'No,' said Lois as she sat beside me. 'I told you so. And now I hate you.'

Chapter Sixteen

Moneymaking Ventures

When a bus came, two minutes later, Lois got on. I didn't even bother to get up to go with her. I'm not speaking to her any more. She hates me. Life sucks, I thought as I watched the bus drive off. At least Lois had her bus pass with her. I had left mine at home and would have to call Mum if I didn't want to walk the two miles to get home. And how was I going to explain that I had no money?

As I was sitting there contemplating my next move, I saw a familiar figure coming across the green towards me. It was that weird headmaster man who'd been so rude to me in the waiting area of the hospital. Last person I want to see, I thought. I pulled the hood of my jacket over my head and looked down at the ground in the hope that he'd keep on going.

'If it isn't our little Zodiac Girl,' I heard him say, moments later.

I kept staring at the ground. 'Nff. Not me. Must be mistaken.'

Dr Cronus sat down next to me. 'How's the wrist?'

I decided that there was no point in hiding. He clearly knew who I was. 'Bit sore still. Why do you ask? Have you come to gloat again?'

Dr Cronus sighed. 'Not at all, my dear. Not at all. No. I like you and I like what you want to do. Mario told me. I've been looking at your birth chart and you're a spunky young thing – I can see that.'

'Yeah. Aries, the movers and shakers of the world.'

Dr Cronus looked at me kindly. It was very unsettling. 'You're feeling dispirited, aren't you?' he asked. 'I have days like that, days when I just feel weary and misunderstood.'

I nodded. 'That's exactly how I feel. I . . . so wanted to do something good. To help at the hospital I was in, but . . . well, everything's gone wrong.'

'Everything?'

'I need a million pounds and what do I do? I lose the only money I had by senseless gambling.'

Dr Cronus burst out laughing. 'See. I knew I'd like you. You're bright. You learn fast and you've learned fast that there are no easy ways to make money.'

'Tell me about it. So. Mario said the people in his planet club will help me. That was the prize. Help. Can you help?'

'Planet club? What planet club?'

'You know. You all pick a planet to be. Nessa's Venus.

You picked to be Saturn. Mario is Mars. Actually, I was wondering about that. On my phone, it says there are ten of you. Is that the whole club? Like what if someone wants to join and also be a Venus planet? What happens then?'

'Oh no, dear. There can only ever be ten of us. One of each. Individual. Unique.'

'That limits your membership, Doctor Cronus. Like, I don't know how you fund your club, but I am sure there are costs. Maybe that's how I could make some money. Advertise your club a bit, get you a few new members – people who like pretending to be a planet like you lot. Sounds like it could be fun. Do you have special nights? You know, when you all get together? Themed dinners? Picnics? That sort of thing?'

Dr Cronus was looking at me open mouthed. 'You don't seem to have quite gripped the situation. We are the living embodiment of the planets. We're not in fancy dress or part of a club. We are the real thing. I am Saturn. I am not pretending to be him.'

Now it was my turn to laugh. 'You're good, Doctor, really good. And I'll play along; I like a game as much as anyone. But, seriously, how can you guys help me achieve my aim?'

Dr Cronus sighed and rolled his eyes. 'To make a million?'

I nodded.

'Start with small steps,' he said. 'Every journey begins with the first step. That's my advice.'

'Small steps.'

'Yes. There are loads of practical things that you could do. You need a plan. Now, have you got a notebook?'

'No.'

Dr Cronus produced one from his pocket. 'Always carry paper. That's another bit of advice. You never know when a good idea might strike. Now. Practical ways to make money. You could wash cars for neighbours on the weekend, that would be a start.'

I looked down at my wrist. 'Not going to be much use at that, am I?'

'You've got one good hand and, anyway, you can delegate. Get a team together. Now, come on, work with me.'

'Er . . . babysitting. People pay good money for that,' I said.

'Now you're cooking,' said Dr Cronus. 'What else?'

'Um . . .'

We spent the next half hour coming up with ideas and, once we got going, I really got into it and in the end we had a good list.

'So what have we got?' asked the doctor when it seemed that we couldn't think of anything else.

I read out the list. 'Cake sale. Candle making. Guess

games – like guess the number of sweets/coins in a jar. Sponsored walks. Raffle tickets for donated prizes. Face painting. Jumble sale. These are really brilliant ideas, but they'd only make peanuts. We'd raise some money, maybe enough to buy a piece of furniture, but never the whole wing. I need the big bucks.'

'This would be a good start and you have to start somewhere.'

I had my doubts. It sounded like a lot of hard work for little return. Dr Cronus seemed to pick up on my thoughts. 'There you go. Impatient as usual. Always wanting everything to happen yesterday.' He stuck out his bottom lip. 'See if I care. If you don't like my ideas, ask one of the others. That is why you have a zodiac phone, you know.'

'It's not that I don't like your ideas, Dr Cronus, but you're not thinking very ambitiously. This is a big project.'

The doctor's lip went out further. 'Ask the others, then. See if I care.'

'Well, Mario hasn't been much good. He keeps saying it has to come from me,' I said.

Dr Cronus looked at the list. 'These ideas did all come from you, well mainly. Got your phone?' I nodded and pulled it out of my rucksack. 'Go on, then. Ask for help.'

I texted in the message:

Need help to raise big bucks.

And pressed SEND TO ALL.

My phone bleeped a few seconds later. It was Mario.

'You have two weeks left,' he said. 'You'd better get on.'

'You are so impatient, Mario,' I said. 'Like most people say, "Hi, how are you?" when they pick up the phone.'

'Hi, how are you and what's your next step?' he asked.

'Um, I'm working on a plan and waiting for some input.'

Dr Cronus nodded and stroked his beard. Moments later, Uri appeared at the end of the concrete path that led across the green. He was on a skateboard and wearing his sci-fi costume again. He whizzed past us.

'Friends,' he called as he balanced on one leg. 'New friends. Unite.'

'Well, he would say that, wouldn't he?' Dr Cronus muttered.

'Why would he?' I asked as I watched Uri stand on his hands on the skateboard and go backwards. He really was an ace performer.

'Uri, Uranus. Rules Aquarius. Aquarians are big on friends and unity.'

'So what did he mean? Oh, don't tell me, only I can

figure that out. Maybe that I have to apologize to Lois. I . . . I guess I can do it. In fact, I'll do it now!' I got out my normal phone and called Lois's mobile. With a bit of luck, she'll pick up on the bus, I thought as I listened to the dial tone.

'It's me,' I said when she answered. 'Please don't hang up. I'm sorry, Lois. I really am. I was a pig making you spend all your money and I'll make it up to you. When Mum gives me my next pocket money, I'll repay you. Honest.'

'No more scratch cards?'

'Heck no. They're for losers.'

I heard Lois laugh at the other end of the phone. 'Mates forever, yeah?'

'Deffo,' I said. I clicked off and gave Uri, who was whizzing past on one leg, the thumbs up. 'Sorted.'

'Is Lois a new friend?' asked Dr Cronus.

I shook my head. 'No. We've know each other for ages.'

'Uri said new friends, didn't he?'

'Did he?'

'He did. So maybe not sorted. Oh, here comes Venus,' said Dr Cronus as the beautician lady from the hospital appeared on the other side of the green. She was dressed in a white tracksuit and was jogging with her blonde hair flowing out behind her.

'The right image will help,' she said as she ran past.

I looked down at what I was wearing. I had on my usual jeans and a blue jacket. So? I was out on a cold grey autumn day. What did she expect? That I wore a tiara? I put my hand up to my head. 'Do you think she means my hair?'

Dr Cronus looked at my head. 'Very possibly.'

'Do you mean my hair?' I called after her.

Nessa turned round and jogged back. She caught her breath then took a good look at my hair, picking up strands and scrutinizing them critically. 'Mmm. Ya gotta do somethin' soon, love. But ya can't risk colourin' again, not after what ya did to it. It might all snap off. And . . . although yer roots are comin' through with new 'air, there's not enough there yet to cut it short without ya lookin' like ya joined the marines. No, best come in the salon one day and I'll do ya a moisturisin' treatment and we'll try to improve the condition. Awright?'

I nodded. I knew that I looked weird – my red roots really stood out against the white colour of the rest of my hair. I'd tried to tell myself that it was an individual look, but even I wasn't convinced. I pulled my baseball cap out of one of the pockets of my rucksack.

'Cover up,' I said as I put it on.

'Good idea and it suits ya,' said Nessa, and off she jogged.

I turned to Dr Cronus. 'Hair advice wasn't exactly

what I meant when I texted that I wanted help.'

'You have to be more specific, then,' he replied.

Next came Selene. Queen of the wackos, I thought as she approached and I saw what she was wearing. She was dressed in a long silver-green ankle length skirt and a blue silk top, and she had her silver-grey hair loose down her back. She beckoned to Nessa who was now on the far side of the green. Nessa went over to her and the two of them began to dance on the green. It was a strange dance that involved a lot of arm waving.

'What the . . . ?' I said. 'They look like a pair of mad hippies.'

Dr Cronus chuckled. 'Do you think I should join them?'

'If you do, I'm leaving,' I said.

Dr Cronus looked put out. 'I can dance, you know. I really can. Just no one ever gives me the chance. Just because I look old doesn't mean I can't move.'

'I know how you feel, Dr Cronus,' I said. 'I was up for a great part in the school show, you know, but because I hurt my arm I can't be in it now. I think the school is prejudiced against people like us.'

'Then why don't you tell them that?'

'Yeah right, don't think I didn't try. Actually . . .' an idea was starting to hatch in my head. 'Hey, you may have something there.'

Dr Cronus sighed wearily. 'I have my uses.'

I didn't hear any more because I was up, on my way home. I had things to do. People to see. Speeches to write.

Chapter Seventeen

School Assembly

I gazed out at the sea of faces in front of me and took a deep breath. This is it, I told myself. My moment to change everything. It was Wednesday morning of the third week of my zodiac month and Mr Simpson, our headmaster, had given me a spot at our school assembly after he'd made the usual announcements. Stay calm, I told myself. And remember to speak slowly. That was what our drama teacher had always told us about doing presentations – that and be prepared. I reckoned I was as ready as I was ever going to be having spent every moment that I could since Saturday on the green with Dr Cronus discussing what I was going to say. Plus I'd done a practice run-through on Monday evening and last night with Lois after school. I was confident that my speech would have the desired result. I'd worded and reworded it so many times. My plan was to appeal to everyone's conscience. People would have to have a heart of stone not to be moved by what I had to say. I was going to get everyone on board with the project to raise money for the new hospital wing. I'd realized while talking things over with Dr C that I couldn't do it on my own. It had to be a group effort involving everyone in the school. I'd coordinate it after I'd inspired everyone in front of me with what I had to say.

Mr Simpson took off his glasses. 'And now one of our pupils, Marsha Leibowitz from Year Eight, has got something that she'd like to say to you,' he said, and he moved aside and indicated that I should step up to the podium. I took a deep breath and walked forward.

'Right. Hi, everyone. So, yeah. About two weeks ago, I had a fall – as you can see.' I held up my bandaged wrist and some wag at the back applauded. I didn't let her put me off and continued, 'I hurt my wrist. I had to spend a couple of nights in hospital. I can tell you it was a real eye opener – I'd never had to stay in one before. Anyhow, what I wanted to say is, it got me thinking. It's very boring in there for a start –'

Halfway down the hall I could see a bunch of girls from Year Nine nudge each other, one rolled her eyes and another made a circular motion with her hand. I knew the gesture. It was one that I used when I thought someone was droning on and I wanted them to wind up. Seeing their reaction threw me for a moment and, looking around the hall, they weren't the only ones who looked uninterested. Quite a few girls were looking out of the windows or around at each other. 'I . . . I am trying, that is, I am going to start a project, or . . . that is . . . a bunch of projects . . .' My confidence faltered and my perfectly planned speech seemed to be deserting me. Suddenly I felt cold inside and flat. I am making a fool of myself, I thought. Everyone looks so bored, as if they can't wait for me to finish and get out into the corridors to chat with their mates. I searched for Lois in the audience and there she was in the usual spot we stood in, three quarters of the way back on the right. Her expression was concerned, but when she saw me look at her she beamed and gave me the thumbs up. I can do this, I told myself. Don't give up now. I just have to make them listen.

'I . . . Just try to imagine how you would feel if you had to go away from your home, away from what is familiar. It's not easy, I can tell you. The days and nights in a hospital can feel very long especially for those who are in there long term.' The girl who had been doing the wind-up gesture made a fist with her right hand, put it up to the corner of her eye, stuck out her bottom lip and made a face like she was crying. Her friends loved it and did the same mock crying act. Just get through it, I told myself. Think of Amy. 'If there was a recreation wing for people in there, a place to go to relax and chill out and forget about illness and being sick and all the anxiety that goes with it, it would be so much easier. We are the people that can make that happen. I'm asking for your help. This Saturday from eleven onwards Mr Simpson has given me and anyone else who would like to volunteer the use of the sports hall. We're going to have a fair to raise money. There will be all sorts of activities you can take part in. Cake sales. Guess the coins in a jar . . .'

I couldn't help but focus on the group of girls from Year Nine. They looked like they were about to have a giggling fit. The one who had rolled her eyes, was now pulling silly faces, crossing her eyes and making a face like she was about to be sick. Oh God, this isn't going well, I thought. 'Um. I've put some forms on the notice board in the main hall. Please sign up and, if you have any great ideas, put them down too. Together we can make it happen.'

I had meant to say the last part in a really enthusiastic voice. It was my slogan. I had put it on top of all the lists and was going to put it on any posters or brochures. Together we can make it happen. But it came out in a whisper.

Mr Simpson stepped forward. 'Well done, Marsha. I like to hear that our girls are taking part in worthy causes.'

The girl from Year Nine silently mimicked what Mr Simpson had said and her friends started giggling again, their shoulders shaking in silent laugher. I knew what they were thinking – that I was a Miss Goody Two-shoes.

That I was a bore. It was what I would have thought just a few weeks ago.

I stepped down from the stage and made my way over to Lois, keeping my eyes firmly down on the ground. This was one time I definitely did not want to be the centre of attention.

Lois and I checked the lists on the notice board every break, every morning and every evening until Friday. At first there were only a few names until a last check on Friday evening showed that the list had suddenly grown. A whole pile of people had signed up.

'Hey, look at this, Lois,' I said. 'I knew people would come through in the end.'

And then I read the names. Paris Hilton. Minnie Mouse. Betty Boo. Jessica Rabbit. Jane Eyre. Tracy Beaker. Harry Potter. Professor Dumbledore. Winnie-the-Pooh. A whole list of fictional names.

'I bet I know who's done this too,' I said to Lois. 'Those girls from Year Nine. Honestly, I'd like to see them spend a few days in hospital with nothing to do. They wouldn't even last an hour.'

Lois squeezed my arm. 'Never mind. It's not over yet. I'm sure a few people will turn up tomorrow. I heard some girls from Year Seven in the cloakroom saying that they were going to come.'

'And I'll text all my new planet friends to see if they will come along. As Mario keeps reminding me, I have just over a week left and he did say that they are here to help.'

'Together we can make it happen,' said Lois. She put up her hand to high five me.

I high fived her back but my heart was sinking.

Chapter Eighteen

Making It Happen?

'I don't really see the point in even going,' I said to Dad as we packed up the boot of the car ready to go to the sports hall.

Dad put his arm round me and gave me a hug. 'Come on, Marsha. This isn't like you. Where's that usual I can do anything attitude of yours?'

Got up and died at school assembly on Wednesday, I thought as I remembered the mixed reception of laughter and boredom and then the fictional list.

Dad punched a fist into the air. 'Together we can make it happen. Yeah?'

'Yeah,' I said, and I stepped back from the car to do a karate leap and kick, if only to keep him happy. 'I am ze Zodiac Girl, hazah!'

Dad laughed. 'And what is that supposed to mean?'

'Me. Aries. According to an astrological Internet site that Lois found, I am this month's Zodiac Girl.'

'Great,' said Dad. 'Go, Zodiac Girl.'

'Go,' I said, and smiled back at him. I didn't want to

admit what a letdown it was going to be today. My family had been so brilliant at supporting my venture I felt embarrassed to tell them that no one was going to show. Mum had spent the last two nights making some colourful A4 posters to stick to the walls outside the school and Dad had taken one of them to his work and photocopied it so that we had a ton of leaflets to hand out. Mum had also been into the local charity shop and asked them if they had any spare jumble. They told her to stop by early Saturday morning and they'd pile her car up high. They seemed glad of the chance to clear their back room. Cissie and Eleanor had surpassed themselves and had spent the last few evenings baking a variety of cakes for the sale. By the morning, they had a great mix of coffee, chocolate fudge, vanilla and Madeira cakes. They got into the back of the car with the goodies balanced on their knees. Oh well, I thought miserably, at least we can eat the cakes between us.

'I'll meet you there,' said Mum, getting into her car.

'Have you got the balloons?' I asked as she started up. She gave me a wave and a nod. 'Check.'

I got into the front of Dad's car and he started up. As we drove off down the road, I gave myself a good talking to. Get a grip, Marsha Leibowitz. You don't normally let things get to you. So what if not many people turn up? Lois and my family will be there and you owe it to them to do your best.

'Together we can make it happen,' I said.

'Yay,' chorused Dad, Cissie and Eleanor.

Lois was already at the hall along with a few of the teachers when we got to school, and I was happy to see that Mrs Pierson and Mr Simpson were amongst them.

'Got to support my girls in ventures like this,' said Mr Simpson. 'Now, what would you like us to do?'

I beckoned him to come round to the back of the car where Dad was unloading a big bowl and a pack of sponges. Mr Simpson looked at me and then the sponges, then back at me. He got what they were for straight away.

'Oh, noooooo,' he groaned.

I grinned back at him. 'I was going to ask Dad to be the victim, but people will pay so much more to throw a wet sponge at their headmaster.' That's if anyone shows, said a voice at the back of my head.

Mum and Lois got busy blowing up balloons and then went outside to tie them to the railings, to put up the posters and to give out leaflets to passers-by. It was an hour till kick off and the streets were empty apart from a car that had just drawn up outside the hall. Five young girls piled out.

'What do you want us to do?' asked a little blonde one.

'We're here to help,' added her redheaded freckly friend.

'Man the jumble,' I said as Mum pulled up in her car. She got out and opened the boot to show us a ton of black bin bags that looked ready to burst. 'That would be brilliant.'

The girls set to it and were soon busy organizing their stall.

Inside the hall, Mrs Pierson called me over to a table where she had set out four jars of jam. 'Not much to show,' she said, 'but you didn't give us much time.'

'Oh, I think I can add to that,' said a man's voice, and we turned to see that Joe from the deli (who liked to play the Jupiter part) had arrived. He pointed out of the window at the white van he'd parked outside. 'I need a few willing hands,' he said, and when another group of Year Sevens arrived through the doors, I sent them out to bring in Joe's contribution. Soon Mrs Pierson's stall was groaning with food: pies, pastries, pickles, tarts and delicious-looking ciabattas stuffed with ham, cheese and tomatoes.

'Hey, look,' said Lois as another group of girls arrived soon after. This time, the girls were from Year Eight, including Carol Kennedy. And then came another group bearing bags of games and books and bric-a-brac.

'Left over from the Summer Fayre,' said Carol as the girls began to put stuff out on a table behind her. 'Mr Simpson told us to get it out of the store cupboards.'

'Thanks, Carol,' I said.

Carol looked awkward for a moment and stared at the floor. 'I wanted to do something to help. I knew how much the part of the Ice Queen meant to you and . . . well, I am sorry about what happened to you. It's really rotten.' She looked up from the floor and smiled. I smiled back.

'That means a lot,' I said. 'And good luck in the part. I'm sure you'll be really good.'

Carol smiled. 'I'll try my best, but I don't think I will be as good as you would have been.'

I felt so touched by what she'd said. It was really generous of her. I'd never have said anything like that to her if I'd been in her shoes. People will never cease to surprise me, I thought as I watched her busy herself with all the others who had turned up to help.

After that, I hardly had time to think as everyone wanted to know what to do, where to set up, what to charge for what. Luckily Mario had arrived and, with Joe from the deli and Dad, he was soon organizing people to do various tasks, like setting up a tea urn, and pouring juices and water to go with the cakes and sandwich stalls. It was ten minutes to opening time and the hall was a hive of activity, chatter and laughter.

Nessa arrived with a couple of her assistants. She gave me a wink then went off to set up a mini beauty salon in the corner of the hall. A board she put up showed that she was offering manicures, mini facials and make-up sessions. I gave her the thumbs up.

Next was Sophie King from Year Nine with one of her mates. She came straight over. 'Good on you, Marsha, for getting this organized.'

I remembered the way I had put her off just before my accident and I blushed. 'I am so sorry about the way I was, Sophie,' I said. 'You were trying to do your best to raise money and I fobbed you off. How did the show go?'

Sophie grimaced. 'We had to cancel it in the end. I couldn't get anyone with any real talent to volunteer. Maybe I'll try another time, but it turned into a total non starter.'

'But didn't you have a hall booked and everything?'

She nodded. 'Yeah, for a week today, in fact, but luckily I didn't lose the deposit because it was snapped up by a record company who are holding a dance competition. Apparently their venue fell through at the last minute so they were grateful to have somewhere to hold it.'

'What kind of dance?'

'Hip hop. Cat Slick Moman is going to be judging it.'

'Cat Slick Moman? The rap artist?' I asked. I wondered if it was the competition that Skye should have been competing in. No wonder she was fed up if Cat Slick Moman was judging it! He was mega.

'Yeah. There are going to be a whole load of celebs

there and Mr Blake. You know – Oliver's dad.'

'Michael Blake?'

'Yeah, he's Cat Slick's agent, apparently. Plus a whole bunch of his rap-artist mates will be there too as they're in town for some convention. Anyway, what do you want us to do?'

'Um . . .' I looked about the hall and saw that the glass jars Dad and I had filled with sweets last night were standing on a table nearby. 'You could get the Guess how many sweets are in the jar game started. Charge a pound a go, winner gets the whole jar.'

'Will do,' said Sophie, and she and her mate went off to get things started.

I glanced at my watch. 'Five minutes to doors open,' I called.

'Ready,' called Lois from the tea stall.

As I watched everyone take their places, I could feel a plan taking seed, straining to burst into flower at the back of my mind. Something. Something – but I didn't have time to think about it any further as people were coming in the door. Even Dr Cronus showed up to do his bit and set himself up in a corner with a board advertising that he could give out homework tips. I gave him a wave and he waved back.

The rest of the afternoon was a blur as more and more people arrived, and when it started raining at around three o'clock even more people came in, eager to find a cup of tea, a dry place and a bargain. I rushed around helping out where I could, sending out for supplies, more tea bags, scones to take the place of the cakes that had all sold, ushering people towards the various stalls. We took a fortune on the game of Throw a wet sponge at Mr Simpson, who by four o'clock looked like a drowned rat.

When the doors shut at four thirty, all the volunteers sighed with relief. We sent Mr Simpson home to have a bath and get warm, then Mum, Mrs Pierson and I collected all the takings and went into the back room to add them up.

Dad brought us mugs of tea and a few pieces of carrot cake with lemon icing, which Cissie had saved for us, and we sat munching while Mum added up the figures.

'And the total is . . .' She looked around, delaying the moment.

'Oh, come on, Mum,' I groaned.

'Five hundred and forty pounds and sixty-five pence exactly,' she said.

'Yahey,' I said as all the assembled clapped.

'Excellent,' said Mrs Pierson. 'That's more than we usually make. Well done, Marsha. Well done.'

OK, so it's not a million, I thought. But it's a start.

Chapter Nineteen

Skye

On the way home, I got Dad to drop me at the hospital. I wanted to see Amy and let her know how the afternoon had gone. When I got to the ward, I saw that she already had a visitor. Skye was by the side of the bed. She looked up and gave me a wave as I approached. Amy looked pale and tired and was lying back on her pillows. Nevertheless, her face brightened when she saw me.

'Hi, Marsha,' she said.

'Hi. How you doing?'

'Same ole. You?'

I held up my arm. 'It's itching like mad. Can't wait to get it off.'

Skye looked down at her foot. 'Me too,' she said. 'I feel like I want to put a stick inside the cast and have a good scratch.'

'Hey, a girl from my school told me about that competition you were up for. Cat Slick Moman's judging?'

Skye grimaced and looked back at her foot. 'Yeah. Bummer. I'll still go to watch but it's going to be hard now that I can't perform. I had a great routine worked out and all and then this.'

'I know how you feel. I was up to play the part of the Ice Queen in our school show. I worked really hard to get it too.' I indicated my hair. 'Even dyed my hair for the part.'

Skye laughed and shot Amy a conspiratorial look. 'We did wonder.'

'I know. It looks really weird. I'll have it cut soon. It just needs to grow a bit first.'

Skye stared at my head. 'You know, it would look really cool if you had it cut short, but spiked it up keeping the roots red and the tips white. It would be totally unique.'

'Mad more like,' I said. 'I hardly take my baseball cap off these days.'

'Show me your routines,' said Amy.

'Our routines?' I asked.

Amy nodded. 'Yeah. Your dance routines.'

Skye made a scoffing noise. 'Yeah right.'

I held up my arm. 'Er, slightly handicapped at the moment,' I said.

'Says who? Oh, come on,' said Amy. 'Do them for me. I don't have to tell you how boring it is being in here in bed all day with nothing to look at but the ceiling. I loved watching you dance last time you were in.'

Skye and I exchanged glances, then she nodded. 'OK. But, Marsha, you go first.'

'But I have no music,' I said.

Skye began to slow clap and Amy joined in. Clap, clap, clap.

'Oh, all right,' I said, and I stood up. 'OK. Um . . . You have to imagine that it's winter. All the trees are covered in snow. And you are lost in the woods.' I turned my back, made myself get into the character of the Ice Queen, cold hearted and royal, then I turned round and went into my routine. At first I felt awkward with my arm strapped up but after a while I got into it and, as the steps came back, it didn't seem to matter. I glanced over at Skye and Amy. Amy looked transfixed and even Skye looked impressed. When I'd finished, I sat back on the end of the bed. 'I know. Rubbish. It's hard to do it with my arm all strapped up.'

Skye shook her head. 'No. No. You're really good, Marsha. Really good.'

'Yeah,' said Amy. 'You can see that you have a natural talent. That was awesome.'

I felt very flattered and grinned back at her. 'You're just saying that.'

'No, I'm not,' said Amy.

I looked at Skye. 'OK. You're next.'

Skye took a deep breath and heaved herself up. 'Hah,' she said. 'This is going to be such a mess, hip hop like you've never seen it before. Um. OK . . .'

She began to hum a rhythm, which I soon picked up and Amy and I began to clap time as Skye went into her routine. It didn't matter that her foot was strapped up and her movements limited. Anyone could see by the way she moved her upper body, that she could dance and she had great attitude, like laid back but street and sharp.

She finished by doing a slow swirl with her crutch, then gave a short bow. Amy and I clapped and clapped. 'Skye, you were fantastic. Really good. You would easily have won if you'd gone in for that competition,' said Amy.

Skye sighed. 'Maybe.'

'There will be other competitions. You can enter them,' I said.

'Yeah. Right back at ya. There will be other shows.'

I sighed. 'Not with guys like Michael Blake and Cat Slick in the audience.'

Just at that moment, my zodiac phone beeped that I had a message. It was from Mario.

Uri said to remind you about new friends.

I looked over at Amy and Skye and texted back.

Yeah. I have new friends.

He texted straight back.

New friends unite.

'Another riddle,' I said, and showed the girls my phone. 'Remember I told you that I won this phone? Well, the guy that runs the website keeps sending me mysterious messages. Like new friends – I guess that means you two, but new friends unite – what does that mean?'

Skye shrugged, but Amy's eyes shone. 'I know. I bet I know,' she said. 'Like what were we just talking about?'

'The show that Skye was going in for,' I replied.

'Missed opportunities,' said Skye.

'That's just it,' said Amy. 'Are they all solo performances in the competition?'

Skye shook her head. 'No, there are all sorts of entries, solo, duos, groups.'

'Duos, groups,' said Amy.

Skye gave her a puzzled look then nodded as if she'd understood something. 'Oh, I think I see where you're going. No. Come on.'

'What?' I asked, then the penny dropped for me too.

Amy nodded. 'You've got the feet, Marsha; Skye's got the arms and the crutch. You can both dance. Oh, come on. You've got to do it.'

I glanced at Skye.

'No way. We'd look insane. The people who enter these competitions are in a different league. We'd be wasting our time.'

'Chicken,' said Amy.

'Chicken? I am not. You don't know what it's like,' said Skye.

'I know that life is short,' said Amy. 'I know that sometimes you have to go for it even when everything seems set against you. What have you got to lose? What do you think, Marsha?'

'I . . . I . . .' I glanced over at Skye. 'I think Amy's right, Skye. What have we got to lose? And, if nothing else, we can draw attention to the fact that the hospital needs funds for the new wing.'

The beginning of a smile was breaking at the corner of Skye's mouth. 'You and me?'

'Yeah. And . . .' I suddenly had the most brilliant idea. 'Yeah. Not just us. I have a few friends who may help out too. Friends who have always wanted to dance. So, yeah. I say, let's do it. You in?'

Skye nodded. 'Nothing ventured, etcetera, etcetera.'

'And, if I'm feeling better,' said Amy, 'I want to come. If this spell in hospital has taught me anything, it's that life is too short to sit around moping when you could be out hip hopping.'

She put up her hand to high five us.

Chapter Twenty

Auditions

'So who are these other friends?' asked Skye when we got outside the hospital after visiting Amy.

'My zodiac chums. Remember I won the phone? Well, another part of the prize was that I got the help of these people who er . . . How can I explain? I think that they're part of a club that likes dressing up, you know? Only they don't exactly dress up, they um . . . pretend to be characters. Oh, I'm not explaining very well. Like some people join clubs where they dress up as characters out of books, other people dress up as knights of old and relive battle scenes, well the zodiac people all pick a planet to be. Something like that.'

Skye raised an eyebrow. 'They sound barking,' she said.

'Yeah, that's what I thought, but they're OK. Like that clown doctor – he's one of them.'

'Oh him? He was good,' said Skye. 'Yeah, I liked him.'

'And the lady that did the pampering sessions, she's another.'

'Yeah, she was OK,' said Skye.

'Well, I was thinking, I only have another week of their help so why not get them into our group as well? Be pretty cool if you and I were out front, but we had this backing group behind us doing some cool dance steps.'

Skye considered the idea. 'Yeah, maybe, but we have a hell of a lot to do in one week, like the choreography—'

I thought back to seeing Selene and Nessa dancing on the green and Dr Cronus hinting that he had always wanted to dance. 'They like to dance and I've seen a few of them move. And we have to decide what to wear, don't you think? Like should we all wear the same thing or dress individually?'

'Same thing,' said Skye. 'Always looks slicker. And, jeez, we need a rap song. We'll never do it in time.'

'I've got the start of one already. It started in my head when we were up in the ward. I thought we could do it about the hospital.'

Skye didn't look enthusiastic. 'Maybe, but who wants to hear about being in hospital?'

'Let's give it a go,' I said, and I began to rap.

'You'd have to be a dummy
To find hospital funny.
Ain't no joke. Choke back a tear.

Don't wanna be here.'

Skye put her head on one side and grinned at me. 'Hey, newbie, that's not bad. You just thought that up? Yeah. I like it.' She started moving her arms and crutches criss-cross as she sang my words. 'Hey, it's OK. Yeah.'

'So if we've only got a week, we should start right away, yeah?'

Skye nodded. 'And I think we should start by seeing your new friends. See if they really can dance.'

'Good plan,' I said, and I pulled out my phone. I texted in a message.

Calling all planets. Now is your chance to dance. Auditions at

'Hey, where shall we have the auditions? I don't want to take them back to my house. My parents and sisters will want to butt in and be in the group too.' I finished the text:

the green at Osbury in one hour's time.

'Ditto. Families, huh? Always want to know what you're up to.'

'I've said the green at Osbury,' I replied. 'It's a good space there and the sky is clear.'

Skye nodded. 'Lead on.'

Dr Cronus was already there by the time the bus that Skye and I had caught from the hospital arrived. He was dressed in a long cloak that covered him from tip to toe.

'Who's the old codger?' asked Skye as I gave him a wave.

'He's actually a headmaster at a local school, but in the zodiac game he plays Saturn.'

'So what's Saturn?'

'The taskmaster of the zodiac, so I guess it fits that he's a headmaster.'

Skye giggled. 'Yeah, but can he dance?'

'We'll see,' I replied. 'Everyone has their chance.'

'Yeah,' said Skye. 'This is so cool. It's like we're going to be the judges on one of those *X Factor*, looking-for-talent programmes.'

'Yeah,' I said. 'I've always wanted to do that. We ought to have buzzers.'

As we made our way over to Dr Cronus, I saw that Uri was coming over on his unicycle.

'There's the clown doctor – Hey!' called Skye.

Uri stood on the seat of his cycle and did a comedy wave like the Queen does. Behind him, I saw that Mario was coming, accompanied by Nessa, the beautician lady.

I leaned into Skye's ear and whispered, 'The clown doctor is Uri for Uranus, and the hunky black guy is

Mario for Mars and the lady is Nessa for Venus.'

'She's beautiful. Should you and I pick planets to be?'

'Um, I don't think it works like that.'

'We have to pick a name for our group, though,' said Skye.

I nodded. 'Yeah. But let's see who's in it first.'

Mario caught up with us and gave Skye a nod. 'So. Auditions? Marsha. What's this about?'

'I'll tell you.' With Skye's help, I got up on the bench at the shelter. 'OK, gather round, everyone. We've had another idea about how to raise money for the recreation wing at the hospital. There's a competition next Saturday night.' I pointed across the green. 'It's being held in the church hall over there and there are going to be some very important people there. Celebrities, agents, but, most importantly, the prize is ten thousand pounds. I know it's not a million and that's what I was hoping to raise, but it's a good start.'

All the gathered nodded as if they approved.

'My friend Skye and I are getting a group together. The type of dance is hip hop. If you want to audition, get in a line.'

All the planet people started pushing and shoving. Dr Cronus was the worst of all.

'Hey, hey,' I called. 'That's no way to behave. OK, Dr Cronus, if you're so desperate, you can go first but stop shoving.'

Dr Cronus looked sheepish, but he did as he was told.

Skye sat on the bench in the bus shelter and I pulled Mario aside. 'I thought that there were ten of you planets? I have ten names listed on my phone. Why haven't I met all of you and why isn't the whole group here?'

'It depends on the individual chart,' Mario replied. 'It depends on which planets are strongly aspected in your chart at the time of you being Zodiac Girl. Some Zodiac Girls meet some of the planets, some meet the others. Everyone here today is here because they are prevalent in your chart. In fact, Jupiter should be along in a moment.'

'You mean Joe, the deli man?'

Mario nodded and, indeed, Joe's tubby figure was soon seen puffing his way across the green. He arrived with a big grin and a basket of goodies, which he proceeded to hand out.

'A troupe can't dance on an empty stomach,' he said, and passed me a cheese and ham sandwich.

'Let's get on,' Skye called from the bench. 'It's going to be dark soon. If it's not your turn, please sit. Dr Cronus, when you're ready.'

Dr Cronus turned his back to us, then flung off his cloak with a dramatic gesture. He turned round. I felt my mouth fall open and I desperately had to resist the urge to laugh. I daren't look at Skye in case I did. Dr Cronus was wearing a deep-pink ballet leotard, cream tights and ballet shoes. He stood up on his toes, did a pirouette, then danced away. He did look funny, because he was very skinny and had the knobbliest knees I had ever seen, but he was light on his feet and did have a certain grace about him. He did a leap to his left, spun round and ended with a curtsey. We all clapped and he looked so pleased with himself as he picked up his cloak and sat with the others.

I leaned over to Skye. 'What do you think?'

'Um, it's not exactly hip hop, but the old codger can move. What do you think?'

'We could give him a chance. Explain that it's a different style of dance to his audition, but I think we should let him join us. He'd be so upset if we turned him down.'

Skye nodded. 'My thoughts too and our group is about giving a chance to people who might not have one.'

'Exactly,' I said, then called, 'Next.'

Joe got up and he beckoned to Nessa to join him. They put their arms round each other like old-fashioned dancers and danced a waltz.

'Nice, but nothing special,' I commented to Skye, and she nodded back at me.

When they had finished, they did low bows. 'Er, thank you,' I said. 'We'll let you know.' The enthusiasm that I'd felt earlier was beginning to fade. We would be a laughing stock. A bunch of fools. Two girls with injuries, an old timer with skinny legs and knobbly knees, a couple who belonged in the 1950s. Oh well, I thought, I doubt if Uri and Mario can be any worse.

'Next,' I called.

Mario got up. He had brought a CD player with him. He pressed START and some rap music began to play. Skye and I clapped along as he began his steps, leading first with his right elbow then shoulder. He was absolutely brilliant, as good as any of the street artists I'd seen on TV. Halfway through the routine he did the splits, then up he bounced as if he were made of rubber. He sprang down lightly on to his hands and danced while doing handstands.

'Ohmigod,' said Skye as he stood on his head and spun round. We were about to start clapping when he got up, ready to do a few more steps. Uri got up and began to dance with him in perfect time, perfectly in the beat, perfectly in tune. They had rhythm, they had attitude, they had charisma.

'Who are these guys?' asked Skye.

I shrugged. 'Dunno. Blooming good, though, aren't they?'

'Awesome,' said Skye. 'The best. We could win with them on our side.'

I grinned back at her. 'I know.'

Chapter Twenty-One

Preparation

'What have we got so far?' asked Skye.

We were sitting on either side of Amy's bed working on the rap song with her after school. Amy was looking good today, with more colour in her cheeks, and was proving to be a whiz at writing songs.

Skye read from the pad of paper in front of her.

'LEDs twinklin',
People sleepin',
Heavy breathin',
Tubes a leakin',
Hi-tech bleepin'.'

She nodded. 'OK, what next?'
'Try this,' said Amy.

'Me silently freakin'.
I want to scream out,
But I know I can't shout.

I'm stuck here alone,
Just want to go home.'

'Brilliant,' said Skye. 'You're really good at this, Amy. OK. Chorus.'

'You'd have to be a dummy to find hospital funny,' we all sang. 'Ain't no joke. Choke back a tear. Don't wanna be here.'

Amy smiled. 'It's sounding good. How are the rehearsals going?'

Skye laughed. 'Apart from Mario and Uri, it's like trying to teach a bunch of kindergarten kids, but they'll get there. The routine is really simple.'

'And it's going to look so good with all of us doing it if everyone can keep in time,' I said. 'Course, my sisters got wind of it and insisted on being in it too, and my mate Lois didn't want to be left out, so the group is growing.'

'What are you all going to wear?' asked Amy.

'Nessa's sorting that,' said Skye. 'She's the beauty lady who came in, remember? She said she could get us a job lot so we'll see tonight.'

'Yeah. We're meeting every night after school because we don't have long to get it together,' I said. 'So, come on, we need another verse. Er . . . how about . . . um . . . Whispers comin' down the hall—'

'Yeah, good,' said Skye. 'And shadows slidin' on the wall—'

'An emergency,' Amy added. 'Thank God it ain't me. Some kid's fighting for life—'

'Me, I got no strife,' said Skye.

'Just feelin' scared,' said Amy. 'Wish somebody cared. We may be sick—'

We were all quiet for a few moments.

'But when all's said an' done,' I continued, 'we still need some fun.'

'And chorus,' said Skye, and she began to click her fingers in time.

'You'd have to be a dummy to find hospital funny,' we all sang. 'Ain't no joke. Choke back a tear. Don't wanna be here.'

'Yay,' I said when we'd finished. 'Read back that last verse, Skye.'

'Whispers comin' down the hall,' she read.

'Shadows slidin' on the wall,

An emergency.

Thank God it ain't me.

Some kid's fighting for life.

Me, I got no strife,

Just feelin' scared,

Wish somebody cared.

We may be sick. But when all's said an' done

We still need some fun.'

'Sounds great to me,' I said. 'Well done, team. Another verse and I think we're just about there.'

After visiting Amy, Dad gave me and Skye a lift to the church hall in Osbury where the competition was going to be held. Luckily for us, Mario had the keys because he taught a self-defence class there a couple of nights a week. The whole crew was there. Dr Cronus (who mercifully was dressed normally this time in trousers and a shirt), Joe the deli man, Nessa, Uri, Lois, Cissie and Eleanor were waiting for us with one new addition: Nurse Cheryl.

'When Amy told me about this, I just had to come. Is it OK?' she asked.

'OK? It's fantastic,' said Skye. 'So, everybody ready?'

Everyone nodded so Skye hobbled over to a CD player in the corner and put in a disc. Seconds later, the hall filled with the sound of hip hop music.

She indicated her foot and her crutch. 'OK, so you all have to be patient with me,' she said. 'We have our own song, but the CD will give us the back beat and then Marsha and I will do our hospital rap over it. OK. I'll run through it then just follow what Marsha and I do.'

She began to march on the spot. 'OK. Everyone, just march, bend your knees, keep it loose. Right, now walk forward, tap, then back.'

Everyone did as she said.

'Now we're going to add some arms. As you walk forward, lift your arms, push out with your elbows leading, one two three, alternate elbows out as if you're jostling someone aside with your elbows. That's it, good. Forward. Now when we go back, I want you to put palm to opposite shoulder as if you're wiping it and turn your face to the shoulder as you do so. Excellent. Looking good.'

It wasn't looking good. No one was in time. Some were wiping when they should be nudging with their elbows.

Skye wasn't put off by the mess in front of her. She persevered. We marched forward, jumped back, arms thrown away, crossed. It looked good when she did it even with her cast on.

'Attitude, attitude,' Skye yelled at us. 'Dr Cronus, you look far too uptight. Go for a cross between, you couldn't care less and don't mess with me. Perfect, Uri. Perfect, Mario.'

We stepped to the right, tapped, stepped to the left, again throwing arms forward in a gesture as if to say, I can't be bothered. I almost got the giggles at one point when I glanced over at Dr Cronus. He was following the steps so earnestly, but kept missing the beat and marching when he should have been jumping and throwing his arms whenever he could.

'OK, last half,' said Skye, 'then we repeat, repeat,

repeat. Walk forward, always starting on the right foot, one two three. Now put your hands on your hips, like you're tucking your thumbs into the tops of your trousers, then back you go, turning your body sideways. Right, now forward again, this time slide to the right, to the left, good. Looking good. Let's take it from the top.'

Over and over the steps we went. Slowly, slowly, everyone caught on and for a few brief seconds here and there, I got a glimpse of how it might look if everyone kept it together.

And then Dr Cronus decided that he wanted to do a solo spot. He sprang on to his hands as if he were going to try breakdancing, cried out in pain and crumpled in a heap on the floor.

'Oops,' I said as Nurse Cheryl ran forward to see if he'd hurt himself.

Chapter Twenty-Two

Showtime

It was the night of the competition.

We were to be on last.

Our crew sat in the audience with the other contestants and their friends and family to watch the performers. We took our seats and the air was buzzing with anticipation and chatter.

Skye nudged me. 'Ohmigod,' she said. 'He's here.'

I turned to see that Cat Slick Moman had just arrived or, should I say, made his entrance. The door burst open and in he came with an entourage of glamorous people behind him. He was dressed in black, had a black bandana on his head and was wearing sunglasses even though it was dark outside. He stopped at the door as if giving us all time to have a good look at him. And we did. Everyone stared. Behind him were two huge bodyguards who looked like heavyweight wrestlers. They were wearing smart dark suits and also had sunglasses on, which they both took off at the same time as they stared around the audience, looking for anyone suspicious. Next came two sets of twins who walked up to Cat Slick and one of each linked his arm in a manner that suggested that we could look but not touch. One set of twins were blonde Barbie types dressed in pink tracksuits, the other set dark skinned and dressed in black. None of them had the flicker of a smile on their face. Now that's the attitude that Skye was talking about, I thought as I took in the expressions on their faces and the way they jutted out one hip.

'I wouldn't like to meet them on a dark night,' I said.

'Yeah. They look like tough cookies,' said Skye. 'But I bet it's all an act, like my cool act.'

I looked at her for a moment and her face broke into a grin. I grinned back at her and squeezed her arm with my good hand.

Cat Slick Moman and his entourage seemed to glide across the floor to the front where they took seats. Cat nodded at Michael Blake who had arrived five minutes earlier with his son, Ollie. Everyone in the hall was staring at their every move, taking in every gesture, me included. I'd never been so close to real live celebrity before.

'This is so exciting,' said Lois as she looked around the hall.

'I know,' I said. 'And Ollie Blake . . .'

'Swoon, swoon,' we chorused.

'. . . keeps looking over,' I finished.

After Cat, a few more famous rap artists arrived, DJ Diggie and Ice Pick Pete. They sloped forward and sat at the front. Just looking at them was giving me butterflies. I couldn't believe in about half an hour I was going to have to get up and perform in front of them!

The show got started swiftly once everyone was seated and the lights went down. The first act was a boy who looked about fifteen. He was dressed in the usual baggy clothes that were fashionable for hip hop back in the 1980s. His music started up and he began to dance. He was good, very good, and Skye and I exchanged anxious glances.

Next up was a group of three black girls and they were completely brilliant, as if they were made of jello, and they ended their act by doing the splits. I glanced over at Dr Cronus who had his arm in a sling and hoped that the girls weren't giving him any ideas about trying the splits himself. He waved with his good hand and smiled. I was growing fond of Dr C. He might be Saturn and a headmaster but he was a trooper.

A few other groups of girls followed and they were all good, but, as the evening progressed, I didn't feel that anyone stood out. They could all dance, but there was nothing unique about any of them.

'I think we might be in with a chance because we're different,' I whispered to Skye.

'Yeah,' she whispered back, then giggled. 'You can say

that again. And, hey, Cheryl hasn't shown up.'

'Maybe she chickened out,' I said. 'Or didn't want to be associated. I wouldn't blame her.'

After an hour, there was a short break for refreshments and I noticed that one of Cat Slick's bodyguards opened up a huge freezer box and handed out bottles of juice to the entourage. I'd read somewhere that he was anti-booze and only drank organic juices.

'We'd better go backstage and get dressed,' said Cissie. 'Nessa has our outfits ready.'

I got up to go and, as I did, Skye nudged me again. I noticed that someone was coming in the door at the back. 'Hey,' I called when I saw who it was. It was Amy and she was with Nurse Cheryl who was pushing her wheelchair. Her mum and dad were behind her and Nurse Cheryl waved when she saw us.

'We're not too late, are we?' she asked when they reached us.

'You've missed the first half, but there are loads of others to go,' I said, and indicated where Skye and I had been sitting. 'Here. Take our places.'

Amy's mum stepped forward at this point. She looked so like Amy with the same brown hair and fine features. 'Actually,' she said. 'We were hoping that Amy could be onstage with you. I know she's in her wheelchair, but maybe she could do the rap song with you.'

I glanced at Skye who nodded.

'Course,' I said. 'Yeah. That would be brilliant.'

'Great,' said Cheryl. 'So let's get ready to boogie.'

Backstage, all our crew were changing into the outfits that Nessa had brought. They were perfect: baggy white tracksuits with a silver stripe up the side of the legs and the arms, white baseball caps – which we all wore backwards – and ginormous white sneakers.

'Hey, Dr C,' I said when I saw him checking himself out in the mirror. 'You look way cool.'

He nodded and turned his baseball cap backwards. 'Yeah. Yeah, I do, don't I?'

'And one last touch,' said Nessa when we were almost ready. We all burst out laughing when she produced bandages, slings and eye patches. 'Help yourselves, guys.'

Everyone fell upon the 'accessories'. Mario went for an eye patch, which rather suited him. Uri went for a bandage that he wound round his middle in a bizarre fashion, but I was starting to get that that was his personality. Nessa bandaged her head and Joe the deli man went for a leg cast and a crutch. Amy went for an arm bandage and my sisters both picked eye patches. I think they wanted to be like Mario – they kept glancing at him and giving him flirty looks. Once we were all dressed and ready, we looked like a right bunch of nutters.

'OK, let's go,' I said, and we left the dressing room and gathered in the wings of the stage along with the other waiting contestants. Skye looked around at our group and got the giggles and that started me off and that started Amy off and soon all of us were holding our sides laughing.

'Shh,' said the MC, so I did my best to straighten my face and focus on the stage. A group of four boys was springing around on their hands, just finishing.

'We can't compete with that,' said Skye.

'Well, Mario and Uri can,' I said. 'No worries.'

As we stood waiting for the stage to clear, I stared out into the audience. My butterflies were all up and flying about inside me like they were trying to escape. Cat Slick and his friends looked totally unimpressed, their faces giving nothing away, although they clapped politely at the end of the performance.

'And now for our last act,' said the lady, who was the event's MC. 'A new group and I'm told that, if they win, they want to donate the proceeds to build a new recreation wing at our local hospital. So let's give a big hand for Accident Prone.' The name had come to me early this morning, and when I put it to the others everyone loved it.

We hobbled on to the stage like a bunch of invalids who could hardly move and the audience began to cheer as we took our positions. Amy took her place to the right of the stage and Dad gave the nod and turned to the CD player. The beat started up. We began to tap our feet, then faced the audience and went into our routine.

Walk forward one two three, back, right elbow up and out left, up and out, right up and out. So far so good. We were all in sync.

As the crew fell into step behind us, Skye and I stepped forward and Amy wheeled herself over to join us. We went into our rap, and I glanced over at Cat Slick. For a moment I almost lost my concentration because he had taken his glasses off, was sitting up straight and had a big smile on his face. Next to him, Ollie Blake was watching me and he was smiling too.

'LEDs twinklin',
People sleepin',
Heavy breathin',
Tubes a-leakin',
Hi-tech bleepin',
Me silently freakin'.
I want to scream out,
But I know I can't shout.
I'm stuck here alone,
Just want to go home,' rapped Amy.

We all joined in with,

'You'd have to be a dummy
To find hospital funny.

Ain't no joke. Choke back a tear.
Don't wanna be here.'

Skye and I fell into step with the others. They were doing brilliantly. Even though we'd rehearsed every night since we'd decided to enter the competition, I'd still had my doubts and wondered if it was going to be a major disaster. But everyone seemed to be totally together. As agreed, halfway through we all stood back and let Uri and Mario come forward. They did their hand springs and head spins and the audience cheered. They loved them. We were about to fall back in when Dr Cronus stepped forward. Oh God, I hope he's not going to ruin everything, I thought as the old man knelt on the floor and attempted to stand on his head. One attempt and he fell back, a second and he lost his balance and then . . . he was up! Spinning! The audience roared their appreciation. He sprang up like a fifteen-year-old, grinning from ear to ear, his sore wrist magically mended, then his knee gave way and he had to hobble back in line. The audience thought it was part of the act and laughed.

We fell back in step, got to the end of the rap and by the last chorus Cat was on his feet rapping the chorus with us. The audience clapped along. People at the back stood. I looked over at Amy and Skye and gave them the thumbs up.

We went into the last steps, forward one two three, bend the knees, wiggle through the body, make a half circle with the right arm, step touch to the left, step touch to the right and we were done.

The wait at the end felt like eternity, but finally the MC stepped up.

'And third position goes to Arthur C.'

The audience clapped as the first boy got up and took his prize.

'And, in second place, Biz Gos and the Goose Girlies.'

The three black girls who did the splits took to the stage.

'And, in first place . . .' She held her breath and I held mine. 'First place goes to . . . Accident Prone!'

The place erupted and everyone got to their feet, including Cat Slick Moman.

We climbed and hobbled up on to the stage and took our bows. This is one of the best moments of my whole life, I thought as I looked out at the cheering crowd and then at my fellow dancers. It couldn't have been more perfect, even if I'd played the Ice Queen. It was better than that because, although I was centre stage, I was there with the team and it felt so good to share the spot.

Epilogue

A month after the competition, Cat Slick Moman released a new single. It was called Hospital Rap and was written by three girls, Amy, Skye and Marsha. It went straight to number one in the charts and raised two million pounds. The girls gave the proceeds to the Osbury Royal Hospital. Building work on the recreation wing for children and teenagers in hospital started soon after.

Amy, Skye and Marsha were booked to cut the ribbon on the opening day. By that time, Marsha's hair was back to normal.

Hospital Rap

LEDs twinklin',
People sleepin',
Heavy breathin',
Tubes a-leakin',

Hi-tech bleepin',
Me silently freakin'.
I want to scream out,
But I know I can't shout.
I'm stuck here alone,
Just want to go home.

You'd have to be a dummy
To find hospital funny.
Ain't no joke. Choke back a tear.
Don't wanna be here.

Whispers comin' down the hall,
Shadows slidin' on the wall,
An emergency.
Thank God it ain't me.
Some kid's fighting for life.
Me, I got no strife,
Just feelin' scared,
Wish somebody cared.
We may be sick,
But when all's said an' done
We still need some fun.

You'd have to be a dummy
To find hospital funny.
Ain't no joke. Choke back a tear.

Don't wanna be here.

Gonna put on a show,
That's the way to go,
Find some folks with cash,
Raise a real big stash
And build a palace of fun
For everyone.
So 'stead of lying around
Wearin a frown
Kids have a place of their own,
A leisure zone,
Some real home from home
To hang out and chill,
Forget they're ill.

Cos you'd have to be a dummy
To find hospital funny.
Ain't no joke.

The Aries Files

Characteristics, Facts and Fun

March 21 – April 20

Confident, daring and spontaneous, Arians are always looking for new challenges. They are natural-born leaders and at their happiest when they can show everyone what they're good at!

An Aries who's not getting her way can be impatient and stroppy, but they make brilliant friends. If you're feeling bored, energetic Aries will always think of something exciting to do!

Element:	Fire
Colour:	Red
Birthstone:	Diamond
Animal:	Ram
Lucky day:	Tuesday
Planet:	Ruled by Mars

An Arian's best friends are likely to be:
Sagittarius
Leo

An Arian's enemies are likely to be:
Cancer
Libra

An Arian's idea of heaven would be:
Being the centre of attention, like the lead in the school play!

An Arian would go mad if:
They were being bossed about by someone – teachers beware!

Marsha's Top Audition Tips

1.**Know yourself!** Choose a character or part that you can identify with, and acting will be easy!

2.**Practice makes perfect!** You HAVE to know your piece off by heart. Don't look at the words unless you go completely blank.

3.**Stand out!** If you wear a bright colour or pattern to the audition you will be remembered, but make sure it's something comfortable. Try not to look too crazy though . . .

4.**Be confident!** But not full of yourself. Nobody

likes a diva!

5.**Smile!** It will make people think that you are fun to work with, and it's harder to be nervous when you smile.

6.**Keep going!** Don't make a big deal of it if you make a mistake, and no one will notice.

Are you a typical Aries?

You're at school and you notice a younger kid being picked on. What do you do?

A) It's none of your business, so you keep out of it.

B) Go over to them later and teach them how to stand up for themselves.

C) March over there and stand up for them. You can't stand bullies.

You've gone to see a movie you've wanted to see for ages. Someone is talking in the cinema behind you. What do you do?

A) Move seats.

B) Complain to the manager.

C) Turn around and give them a piece of your mind! Shu-ut UP!!!

You're having a party and no one's dancing! What do you do?

A) Try to persuade your best mates to get on the dance floor.

B) Decide that your party is a failure and have a tantrum.

C) Jump on the dance floor and show everyone your latest moves. You love to show off!

You go shopping for a great party outfit. What do you choose?

A) Something simple, classic and black. You can't go wrong!

B) Whatever is the height of fashion. You wouldn't be seen dead in anything else.

C) Something wild to get you noticed – in the brightest colour possible. You can start a new trend.

Your mum and dad have finally given in and said you can have a pet. What do you go for?

A) A puppy – you want something loyal and cuddly.

B) A kitten – like you, it's independent and strong-willed.

C) A snake – you'll be the talk of the school!

You see a group of girls in the playground chatting and looking over at you. What do you think?

A) They are just having a chat and looking around to see who is about.

B) They are probably talking about some TV programme they saw last night.

they saw last night.

C) They are talking about you. Doesn't everyone?

How did you score?

Mostly As – almost Aries
Your Aries personality is in there somewhere, you just need to let it out . . .

Mostly Bs – agreeably Aries
You've got loads of great Aries qualities – don't be afraid to show them off!

Mostly Cs – amazingly Aries
Wow – you know what you want and you know how to get it! You're Aries to a T.